That couldn't be her.

Jessica Moran had been pudgy and hopelessly homely. The woman who emerged from the flowers was as lithe as a wood sprite. And when she saw him her eyes went very wide. Then she glanced over her shoulder, looking like a deer who wanted to bolt.

"I'm hoping you can help me," he said. "I'm looking for—"

But the words didn't come. He felt the shock of her eyes. They were the kind of eyes a man never forgot, ever.

Even way back then, when she had been a few pounds overweight and plain, he'd looked into her eyes and felt enchanted.

Enchanted enough to say, "I'll call."

And, of course, then he'd come to his senses. And never called.

He could see the memory of that long-ago promise not kept flit through the clear surface of her eyes, and he knew why she had wanted to run.

It wasn't because she thought he was a stranger. No. It was because Jessica Moran knew exactly who he was.

Dear Reader,

If you can't beat the summer heat then join it! Come warm your heart with the latest from Silhouette Romance.

In *Her Second-Chance Man* (SR #1726) Cara Colter enchants us again with the tale of a former ugly duckling who gets a second chance with the man of her dreams—if only she can convince him to soften his hardened heart. Don't miss this delightful story of love and miracles!

Meet *Cinderella's Sweet-Talking Marine* (SR #1727) in the newest book in Cathie Linz's MEN OF HONOR miniseries. This sexy soldier promised to take care of his friend's sister, and he plans to do just that, even if it means *marrying* the single mom. A hero's devotion to his country—and his woman—has never been sweeter!

Talk about a fantasy come to life! Rescued by the handsomest Native American rancher this heroine has ever seen definitely makes up for taking a wrong turn somewhere in Montana. Find out if her love will be enough to turn this bachelor into a husband in *Callie's Cowboy* (SR #1728) by Madeline Baker.

Lilian Darcy brings us the latest SOULMATES title with *The Boss's Baby Surprise* (SR #1729). Dreams of her handsome boss are not that strange for this dedicated executive assistant. But seeing the confirmed bachelor with a *baby?* She doesn't believe it…until her dreams begin to come true!

We hope you enjoy the tender stories in this month's lineup!

Mavis C. Allen
Associate Senior Editor

Please address questions and book requests to:
Silhouette Reader Service
U.S.: 3010 Walden Ave., P.O. Box 1325, Buffalo, NY 14269
Canadian: P.O. Box 609, Fort Erie, Ont. L2A 5X3

Her Second-Chance Man

CARA COLTER

SILHOUETTE *Romance*®

Published by Silhouette Books

America's Publisher of Contemporary Romance

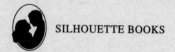

SILHOUETTE BOOKS

ISBN 0-373-19726-8

HER SECOND-CHANCE MAN

Copyright © 2004 by Cara Colter

This edition published by arrangement with Harlequin Books S.A.

® and TM are trademarks of Harlequin Books S.A., used under license. Trademarks indicated with ® are registered in the United States Patent and Trademark Office, the Canadian Trade Marks Office and in other countries.

Visit Silhouette Books at www.eHarlequin.com

Printed in U.S.A.

Books by Cara Colter

Silhouette Romance

Dare To Dream #491
Baby in Blue #1161
Husband in Red #1243
The Cowboy, the Baby and the Bride-to-Be #1319
Truly Daddy #1363
A Bride Worth Waiting For #1388
Weddings Do Come True #1406
A Babe in the Woods #1424
A Royal Marriage #1440
First Time, Forever #1464
*Husband by Inheritance #1532
*The Heiress Takes a Husband #1538
*Wed by a Will #1544
What Child Is This? #1585
Her Royal Husband #1600
9 Out of 10 Women Can't Be Wrong #1615
Guess Who's Coming for Christmas? #1632
What a Woman Should Know #1685
Major Daddy #1710
Her Second-Chance Man #1726

Silhouette Books

The Coltons
A Hasty Wedding

*The Wedding Legacy

CARA COLTER

shares ten acres in the wild Kootenay region of British Columbia with the man of her dreams, three children, two horses, a cat with no tail and a golden retriever who answers best to "bad dog." She loves reading, writing and the woods in winter (no bears). She says life's delights include an automatic garage door opener and the skylight over the bed that allows her to see the stars at night.

She also says, "I have not lived a neat and tidy life, and used to envy those who did. Now I see my struggles as having given me a deep appreciation of life, and of love, that I hope I succeed in passing on through the stories that I tell."

Jessica's Love Potion Ingredients
(for enchanting Brian)

Jasmine: The intoxicating power of jasmine has long been recognized by the perfume industry. In North America the sweetly scented *evergreen jasminum polyanthum,* with its cascades of white flowers, is the most common type. Jasmine is believed to stimulate the brain to create greater awareness. ✓

Rose oil: The most ancient ingredient for love potions, Romans made love on beds covered in rose petals. It is believed that *attar of roses* is the scent Cleopatra used to lure Mark Antony to her bed. The best roses for love potions are believed to be the older hybrids that bloom only once a year. ✓

Peppermint: Peppermint is still a popular ingredient in herbal teas, and it is thought to stimulate great passion. ✓

Coriander: Medieval potions containing coriander were served to the bride and groom on their wedding night as an aid for happy and productive nocturnal activity. The herb also played a starring role in the classic tale *The Arabian Nights.* ✓

Chapter One

For an awful moment, Brian thought the puppy had died.

He glanced at his niece, sitting on the passenger side of his 1964 orange Ford pickup truck. Her hair—dyed an unlikely shade of black—fell in a limp veil, shielding her profile from his probing gaze. Beneath the thin straps of a tank top—also black—her bony shoulders were hunched forward as if she was protecting herself from a blow.

Even after six months of sharing a house with one, Brian Kemp—a bachelor—was no expert on the mysteries of teenage girls. He had been told they were remarkably re-silient, and yet his niece, bent over that puppy with her hands quiet and tense in the golden fur, did not seem re-silient. In fact, he was not sure if he had ever seen a more fragile sight.

He didn't realize he had been holding his breath until the dog drew in a long ragged gulp of air, and then he did, too.

"Are we there?" Michelle whispered, with none of that normal, I-don't-give-a-damn-about-anything hardness in her voice.

"Nearly," he said, hoping it wasn't a lie. He hoped he had remembered the correct turnoff. There were many such turnoffs between Victoria and Duncan, cutting inland away from the ocean. Telling her that he knew someone who might be able to help had been a dumb and desperate measure.

Now they were on this dirt road lined with heavy timber, in the embrace of deep forest. The timber thinned and then gave way unexpectedly. The road was lined on either side with roses. The bushes were huge, with flowers—a cascade of pink and yellow and red. Brian didn't remember the roses. He thought it might have been winter when he last ventured down this road.

But now, in the last days of June, the flowers bloomed in untamed abundance. Their intoxicating scent poured through the open truck windows, wrapped around him, and filled him with the most dangerous of things—hope.

The vet had said to forget it. The puppy was not thriving. He would not live. He had recommended a merciful end.

Michelle had turned away at that pronouncement, tears spilling black down her cheeks as their hot saltiness melted her heavy-handed mascara. Brian had tried to touch her and take the puppy, but she had closed her body around it like a shield, refusing to part with it or be comforted. She had rushed by him and gone to sit in the truck.

Brian Kemp was not a man who asked favors of the universe.

But at that moment, watching through the window of the vet's office as his niece sat hunched in the truck, he realized that she was still such a child—barely thirteen—and he felt a sense of failure and helplessness that were not totally unexpected. Hadn't he known right from the start that he was probably not a good choice for the job of guardian? He had a track record of failing to bring happiness to the female of the species.

He was a cop, and even though Victoria was not a huge city—with a population of only 300,000—Brian dealt with his fair share of tough and terrible stuff. That was his job. He considered himself good at it. His lack of sensitivity was something he'd considered an asset in his life—right up until now. Now he realized that nothing about handling tragedy and chaos on a nearly daily basis had given him even the smallest inkling of how to handle a young girl's breaking heart.

So, standing alone at that window, he had been humbled and amazed to find himself saying out loud, just as if something or someone was listening, "I don't know what to do."

It was a horribly hard admission for a man to make. But especially for one who prided himself in knowing how to take charge of even the most disastrous of situations. The truth was that most of the disasters he dealt with weren't in any way personal. In fact, he was something of an expert at avoiding anything that smacked even slightly of the R word—as in relationships.

A man with no track record when it came to others did not a good guardian make. But six months ago his niece had been orphaned when her parents—Brian's brother Kevin and Kevin's wife Amanda—had been killed in a car accident. Brian was Michelle's only living relative. She'd arrived, not as the little girl of Brian's once-a-year Christmas memories, but as a young woman full of the hostility that comes from losing too much.

A desperate man, Brian had surprised her with the puppy

two weeks ago, hoping it might give her something to do over the quickly approaching summer holidays and, deep inside he hoped it might be some sort of answer to the problems in their relationship. It had looked like it might, too.

After pretending indifference for five minutes, Michelle had named the golden retriever O'Henry, and the pair had become inseparable. The dog slept tucked under her arm. Brian caught her trying to smuggle it in her bag to school. Sometimes he heard her laughing, and it wrenched his heart that she wouldn't do it in front of him, as if laughter was something she needed to feel guilty about.

Now, this tiny puppy, the life preserver Brian had tossed to his niece, was going to be taken from her, too?

"So, if you know what to do, show me. Please," he had said, and then frowned at how the words sounded suspiciously like a prayer. His frown deepened when a memory tickled his mind. Of another girl, a very long time ago, bent over another dog.

She might not even live down this road anymore. It had been at least fourteen years since he had been here. They had both been in high school. A lot could happen in that many years.

The road opened abruptly into a clearing, and Brian felt his mouth drop open. It was the same place, but transformed, whether by season or by time he was not entirely sure.

The road of his memory had not ended in a place like this. This road, the one his desperate heart had led him down, ended in enchantment.

The clearing was filled with flowers, topsy-turvy, cascading, peeping, climbing. Long grasses were braided with dainty yellow blooms. There were clumps of reds and oranges, towers of blues and indigos. He recognized some of them—the deep purple of Canterbury bells, the sassy white of daisies—but most he could not name. Colors, wild to mild, danced together, and scents sweet and sharp mingled, tickling his nostrils and his mind.

Off to the side of the blissful abundance and embraced by the deeper greens and shadows of towering cedars, was a cottage. It squatted on a stone foundation, small, steep-gabled, green, blending into the space around it.

Even Michelle momentarily forgot her distress over the puppy. "Oh-my-god," she said, her favorite expression. "It's awesome."

"You almost expect seven little men to come trundling out, don't you?"

He'd managed to say the wrong thing again, because his niece shot him the ever popular you-are-hopeless look. Did she think he had mistaken her for a baby because of the reference to Snow White? He wanted to ask, to try and cross this minefield between them, but she had already fenced him out and returned her attention to O'Henry.

A miniature pickup truck—red and shiny—marked the parking area, which was a half-circle of gravel. Brian pulled in beside the vehicle and cut the engine. Bird song, riotous with joy, filled the air. A butterfly flew in one window of the truck and out the other. He watched its crooked, floating flight.

"Is that her?" Michelle asked.

He turned his head toward his niece. She was looking out the near window and he followed her hopeful gaze. Then, despite the tranquility of the scene, he felt his own heart plummet.

So, she was not here. He should have guessed that fourteen years was too long to expect a person to stay in one place. He should have guessed that a new owner, with an eye for creating beauty and a green thumb, had taken over. He should have guessed that his memory of a hardscrabble little cottage and weed-filled acres had been more accurate.

For that couldn't be Jessica Moran, rising out of the flowers with her straw sunhat askew.

Jessica had been a short, pudgy girl, hopelessly homely, her hair a peculiar shade of red that had hung long, with untamable bumps and waves in all the wrong places.

The woman who emerged from the flowers was as lithe as a woodland sprite, her naked shoulders slender, tanned and toned. She wore a white sleeveless tank that molded to her small shapely chest and hugged the line of her flat tummy. She had on those pants that men didn't quite get—something between shorts and slacks that ended just above a shapely calf.

Capris, he remembered Michelle correcting him with a roll of her eyes when he had called them pedal pushers.

The slacks were white, too, or had started out that way, but were now smudged dark at the knee.

The woman took off her hat as she came toward them, and her short hair sprang free and danced around her head in a fury of cheerful-looking auburn curls.

She had a basket over her wrist that overflowed with freshly cut flowers and greenery. Under different circumstances, he might have appreciated her loveliness and that of the scene a great deal more. But all he could think now, was, *It wasn't her.*

He got out of the truck, and she skidded to a halt. Her eyes went very wide, and then she glanced over her shoulder, looking like a deer who wanted to bolt back into the safety of the deep green forest that surrounded this little meadow.

He was a big man, and he knew his size could be intimidating, especially to a woman who was in the middle of nowhere and not within shouting distance of a neighbor.

"Sorry to bother you, ma'am," he said, and leaned against his open truck door. He let it provide a slight barrier between them, making no move toward her and keeping his voice deliberately deep, calm and soothing. "I'm hoping you can help me. I'm looking for…"

But the words didn't come. She tilted her chin and moved toward him again. He stopped speaking and studied her, feeling the shock of her eyes. They were green and deep, as refreshing as a midsummer dip in a calm, forest pool. They were the kind of eyes a man never forgot, ever.

Even way back then, when she had been a few pounds overweight, plain and beyond the pale of the high school hierarchy, even then he had looked into her eyes and felt enchanted.

Enchanted enough to say, "I'll call."

And, of course, then he had come to his senses. And never called.

He could see the same memory of that broken promise from long ago flit across the clear surface of her eyes, and he knew why she had wanted to run.

It wasn't because she thought he was a menacing stranger. No, it was because Jessica Moran knew exactly who he was.

But she still moved toward him, halting close enough that he could smell the spice and lemon scent of her above the flowers. She squared her shoulders, pointed her chin, and came forward the final few steps, grace and confidence having swept away the clumsy, awkward girl he remembered. She hooked the basket over her forearm and extended her hand.

Her face was narrow, elfin, and dominated by the huge, soulful pools of her unforgettable eyes. Freckles dotted her nose. Surely, she had not always had lips like that, as plump and inviting as a ripe strawberry?

"Brian," she said, and her voice was clear and melodious. Now he remembered her voice, too, remembered how it had been part of the enchantment. "I was so sorry to hear about your brother and Amanda."

Her hand in his was small but surprisingly strong. He felt the oddest desire to linger over the handshake and explore the energy coming from her, but she pulled her hand back after the briefest of touches.

He recalled that his sister-in-law, Amanda, had been in the same grade as Jessica at high school. He could not imagine that Amanda, or her best friend Lucinda, had ever offered Jessica anything except small, not-so-subtle cruelties.

Lucinda was the girl who had kept him from ever making that call.

Something about Jessica's graciousness made his voice stick in his throat. He now remembered things that he should have remembered long before coming down this road.

"Jessica," he said, finally finding his voice and trying to hide his discomfort and his shock at her amazing metamorphosis. "I didn't recognize you."

"I'm sure I've changed a good deal since we last saw each other. What brings you here?" Polite, but nothing more.

He hesitated. Now would be the time to admit that he'd made a dumb error and just head on back down her driveway. Instead, he heard himself saying, "Do you remember that time I hit that dog at the end of your driveway, and we brought it here?"

Something flickered behind her eyes—it looked suspiciously like pain—and she nodded, a trifle curtly.

He cursed himself for coming here, for following a desperate whim.

He was glad that Michelle chose that moment to slide from the truck, her little bundle cradled in her arms, her eyes huge, begging. "Can you fix my puppy?"

Jessica gave him a startled look and then turned to the girl. Her eyes widened and she held out her hands. Michelle surrendered the weak puppy, and Brian could not help but frown remembering how his niece had refused to turn it over to him.

Jessica took the puppy, and he could see the tenderness of her touch as she cupped its body, ran her hands over it and then rested them above a heart beating too rapidly. She closed her eyes, and when she opened them she shot him another look. He saw a flash in their green depths.

Anger.

Not that he could blame her. He had come with an impossible task. He had placed her in a terrible situation. He could see, from the tiny muscle working frantically in her jaw, that she did not hold out much hope for the dog, and that she knew it was really a young girl's heart that he had placed in her trust.

But there was none of that anger as she turned and with a movement of her shoulder invited Michelle to follow her down the winding cobblestone path that led to the cottage.

Tiny purple violets grew among the cobbles and every time he crushed one under foot he was enveloped in the soft fragrance of it.

"I'm Jessica," she said over her shoulder to his niece. Her voice could have coaxed wild birds from their nests. "You look so like your mother, Amanda. I knew her in high school. She was beautiful, and so are you."

He realized he'd been so thrown off balance by the appearance of the new and improved Jessica Moran that he'd forgotten introductions.

Jessica's tone was so genuine that Michelle blushed and preened despite herself.

The sad truth was that his niece was far from beautiful, especially given her fondness for too much makeup. She dyed her hair that bleak shade of black. She was too thin, and she was having an outbreak of acne.

And yet Jessica's tone made him look at his niece again. He saw something different than he had ever seen before. The deep blue of her eyes, the sweep of her cheekbones, the slender column of her neck.

He felt his hackles rise. Was Jessica that much of a magician that she could make a man see things? Or was he just looking harder since he had obviously made such a poor judgement about Jessica herself in those awkward years of adolescence?

"This is my niece, Michelle," he said belatedly.

"My dog's name is O'Henry." Michelle gave him a look that said the dog was the important one and Brian had gotten it all wrong. So, what else was new? As far as he could tell he hadn't gotten one thing right since his niece had arrived. With the notable exception of the dog.

"After the writer?" Jessica asked.

Writer? He looked between the two females, baffled.

"Yes!" Michelle looked thrilled. So, Jessica got it right, first try.

Brian had assumed the dog was named after a brand of

chocolate bar. He'd gone so far as to assume that Michelle liked them. He'd bought her one and slipped it into her lunch as a surprise. Another obvious error, since the lunch kit came back with the small gift of chocolate untouched.

"What do you like best by him?" Jessica asked. "No...let me guess. *The Gift of the Magi?*"

"Oh," Michelle breathed, delighted. Something leaped in the air between his niece and Jessica, and the hackles on his neck rose again.

Back in high school they had called Jessica a witch and a weirdo. But he had known the truth, even though he had not come to her defense. She was not a witch, or a weirdo. Nor was she a magician.

She was a healer.

He had the uneasy feeling that he had not come here for the dog. In some way he did not fully understand, his request for help had brought him here.

For his niece.

And just maybe for himself.

He snorted out loud at the fanciful turn of his thoughts. He blamed it on the garden, the birds, her eyes and then shrugged the thoughts away before the unwelcome and less than pragmatic way of looking at things had a chance to attach itself to him, like a burr to the underside of a hound.

A perfectly wonderful day, ruined, Jessica thought, cupping the nearly lifeless body of the puppy in her hands as she pushed open the back door to her cottage with her shoulder.

Brian Kemp. Her very worst nightmare had now come back into her life. And how dare he be better looking than ever?

He was more somber now. The boyish recklessness had

been chased from him. And he had lost all that adolescent slenderness and become the man whose promise she had seen a very long time ago. His chest was deep and powerful. His arms rippled with well-formed muscle. His legs were long and straight, the hardness of them evident even through the soft fabric of old jeans.

That dark swatch of brown hair still threatened to fall over one eye, and his eyes remained a place of mystery, as brown as melted chocolate, hinting at a depth that had not material-ized when he was a boy. Jessica refused to give in to the sub-tle seduction of contemplating whether it had materialized later in his life.

His mouth, then, had always had a faint curve upward, as if he were ready to laugh. Now she noticed how the line of it was hard, the upward quirk missing. There were other lines in his face: squint lines around his eyes, the start of a furrow in his forehead.

And yet, if anything, he was even more handsome than he had been in youth. Something in those lines suggested great strength and character. But, of course, she had mistakenly thought she had seen those qualities before.

Jessica glanced around her kitchen and repressed a sigh. The cottage was old, and her attempts to spruce it up by painting the cabinets a delicate shade of periwinkle blue and stripping the wide oak boards of the floor and refinishing them did not hide the fact that the cupboards had gaps and the floors sagged.

Plus, this area doubled as her office and the work area for her mail-order seed and herb business. Drying plants hung up-side down from the ceiling. Heaps of mint and sage crowded her countertops and kitchen table. Her mismatched chairs, one painted yellow, one bright red, had been pulled back from the scarred wooden table so she could move around it easily. The desk in the corner—an antique rolltop and the only really decent piece of furniture in the room—was almost lost under stacks of orders and paperwork.

If a person was trying to impress, this room would probably not forward their cause. But Jessica could not remember the last time she had felt the need to be anything but herself.

She had left that painful teenage world—full of angst, self-doubt and pain—so far behind her that it was easy to imagine it had never existed.

Until a six-foot-something reminder appeared in her driveway. She was pretty sure that was even the same truck.

"Why did you bring O'Henry here?" she asked the girl, keeping every hint of her resentment for Brian's unexpected and unwelcome reappearance in her life from her voice.

The child reminded her of a bird with a broken wing, hurt and fear broadcasting past the mask she had painted on her face.

"My uncle said he had seen you do a miracle once." Her voice was more that of a child who still believed in the impossible than a young woman who had lost so much.

A miracle? How could Brian bring this poor sweet, damaged child here with such an expectation?

Despite her irritation with him, Jessica kept her tone light. "If I had those kind of powers, I would have turned your uncle into a toad."

The girl regarded her steadily, and then asked, deadpan, "You mean you didn't?"

Despite the gravity of the situation, or maybe because of it, a little giggle escaped Jessica. And then Michelle. And then they were both laughing.

"Hey, I don't find that funny."

Which, of course, only made them laugh harder.

Brian tried to look insulted, but Jessica could tell he was relieved to hear his niece laugh. She didn't like the small ripple of tenderness this made her feel for him.

How nice it would be if he just remained the black-hearted popular boy who had promised to call the school's worst social misfit and then reneged.

But he seemed so much more human now, than he had been then, far less godlike. His eyes, in the light of her kitchen, had a deep sorrow in them. And it was evident, from the sideways glance at his niece and the puppy, where those furrows on his forehead were coming from.

He had lost his brother and his sister-in-law and had become an instant parent to a teenager. Life extracted revenge, but somehow she found no comfort in the fact that he had suffered.

Jessica cleared a space at her table and made a nest for the puppy in an old towel. Michelle crowded close to her. "The vet told me he didn't want to live," she whispered, and Jessica glanced at her to see her shoulders hunching. Her voice cracked as she continued, "How could he not want to live when I love him so?"

If only love had the power to make things as a person wished, Jessica thought, and despite herself sent a sideways look at Brian.

Years ago, as a lonely high school senior who had fit in nowhere, she had fallen in love with popular, gorgeous Brian Kemp. But all the force of that love could not persuade him to do the thing he had promised. One small phone call.

A chance. She had been sure that, if given a chance to show him who she really was, he would love her. Instead, he had loved Lucinda Potter, or so it had seemed from the hungry kisses Jessica had witnessed them exchanging behind the Coke machine in the main foyer.

Instead, she reminded herself briskly, he had given her the best of opportunities. She had learned very young that she would have to love herself. No prince riding in on a white charger could make her life wonderful, she would have to do it. And she had done just that.

And now, she had to share some of that wonder with this troubled young girl and never mind the man who had brought her.

"The vet was wrong," Jessica said firmly. "Every creature *wants* to live. Even a bug."

"That's what I thought," Michelle said, her voice stronger.

Jessica closed her eyes and tried to clear her mind. It was a more difficult task than normal. Her kitchen seemed far too tiny with Brian's bulk in it. Over the powerful scents of mint and sage, she could feel his restlessness and detect his presence.

Powerful. Masculine.

She opened her eyes to see him prowling restlessly, looking at her plants and jars with a scowl on his face.

"Brian, why don't you wait outside for a minute?"

Rather than looking insulted, he looked relieved. She felt his energy leave the room with him.

She composed herself after he left by taking a deep steadying breath. She held her hands above the small, dangerously-close-to-death dog. Slowly, her mind emptied of all thought and filled with pure and brilliant light, a spectrum of colors, dancing. Her fingertips began to tingle. All else faded, except the energy moving between her and the puppy.

Finally, she opened her eyes and gazed down at the little dog. She touched him with great and reverent affection.

"Is he going to live?" Michelle asked.

"I don't know," she said, unwilling to give the girl false hope. "But there are a few things I'd like to try. I'll give him some of this." She chose a small jar from a case of them and squeezed a few drops into his mouth.

"Is that like medicine?" Michelle asked.

"Something like that. We'll pick some fresh herbs from the garden and make him his own concoction."

Brian was outside, sitting on her favorite bench. Someday, there would be a small pond there. The rocks and mortar waited there for her to find the time and the energy to undertake such a big project.

Meanwhile, Jessica could only hope the memory of his sitting there—his handsome face lifted to the sun, his hair touched by the wind, his posture so relaxed—was not going to spoil that spot for her.

He didn't appear to notice them, and so she took Michelle to her herb garden and began to pick, explaining each plant carefully to the surprisingly eager young student.

"Well?" he said, coming up behind them, quiet and graceful for such a large man.

"It's too soon to say," Jessica said, with a shrug. "I'd like to keep him for a day or two."

"What's wrong with him? What can you do for him that the vet couldn't?"

"There are many possibilities," she said stiffly. *Why had he come here if he planned to scoff and be cynical?* "You are, of course, free to take him back to the vet if you want."

"No!" Michelle said, and gave Brian a look that could have stripped paint. "The vet wanted to put him to sleep."

He looked between the two of them, and Jessica had the

feeling he was deciding she and Michelle made a dangerous combination. Her suspicion was confirmed by his next words.

"Michelle, how about if we leave O'Henry with Jessica? We'll come back in a day or two and see how he's doing." He correctly interpreted the black look he was being given by his niece. "Of course, we'll phone."

It was written on his face that he was sorry he had ever come here, a regret that Jessica mirrored exactly. Her life was so nice, now. Predictable. Stable.

A man like Brian Kemp could turn that upside down without half-trying.

She waited for him to take his niece and go, but to her bemusement Michelle folded her arms over her chest and planted her legs in a fashion that gave her a surprising amount of presence.

"I'm not leaving."

He ran a hand through his hair, looking at his watch. "Look, Michelle, I have to be at work in an hour, okay?"

"I'm not going anywhere," the child announced, her resemblance to her uncle pronounced with her face set in those stubborn lines. "I'm staying right here with O'Henry. And Jessica."

Chapter Two

"Get in the truck." Brian's voice was low and dangerous. Jessica had heard he was a policeman in Victoria; his voice held deep and unquestionable authority.

His niece, however, looked unimpressed. "No."

Jessica knew now would be a good time to insert herself in the argument and tell Michelle she had to leave with her uncle. But she was no saint and to see the man who had humiliated her suffer at the hands of his headstrong niece was just a little bit satisfying.

In fact, Jessica had to stifle a laugh after seeing the look on Brian's face. He obviously wanted nothing more than to pick up his ninety-pound niece and toss her in the truck. The lines of his face were chiseled with irritation. On any other man it might have marred his good looks, but not on Brian. With his brows lowered like that, and the line of his mouth grim, he had the look of a warrior.

Still, under the fierce mask, Jessica sensed something rather astonishing. Brian was purely, helplessly baffled. Despite the fact that he looked like the most self-composed man ever born—one who could handle anything life threw at him—he was at a total loss when it came to dealing with his five-foot-one-inch niece.

Tell Michelle to go with her uncle, Jessica ordered herself. She wanted Brian out of her space, the quicker the better. On the other hand, she didn't feel inclined to make his life any easier, wonderful life lessons owed to him aside. Surely it wouldn't hurt to stay on the sidelines and let them settle their own argument? Finding his helplessness mildly entertaining was only human, not mean-spirited.

"You can't just stay here with a complete stranger," Brian said to Michelle, "Not that you've been invited. And I have to go to work. So, march."

"She's not a complete stranger," Michelle said.

On very short acquaintance Jessica knew Michelle to be the girl least likely to *march* anywhere, but she offered no comment.

"I don't know the first thing about her," he said, his patience obviously thinning even more. A muscle working in his jaw showed the fine, strong line to perfect advantage.

His niece was just as obviously not about to be intimidated by the facts, or by him. "You do so know the *first* thing about her. You knew where she lived. You knew her name. You knew…"

"Nothing important about her," Brian interrupted, aggravated.

"Like what?" Michelle asked, her voice challenging.

The debate raged in the darkness of his eyes—reason with

her, or put her in a choke hold? Reason won out, but not by much. It was evident he was not a man accustomed to having his authority questioned.

"I don't even know if she's married. I don't know what she does for a living," Brian said.

Jessica pondered what it meant that he wondered that about her *first*. She had not had to debate whether or not he was married. He wore no ring, but it was something more that gave away his single status. He looked like one of those men who have developed an allergy to relationships, carrying his independence around himself like an invisible shield. She was willing to bet that his most successful one was with his truck, which seemed to be the same one he had driven in high school.

Not exactly observations that painted him in a sympathetic light, though he also had the look of a man beleaguered. He was absolutely alone with the challenge of his niece, and it showed.

"She's not married," Michelle said. "Did you see any signs of a man inside that house? Size ten muddy boots at the back door? Smudgy handprints around the light switches? Dishes in the oven? Laundry waiting to be folded in the living room? Root beer rings on the coffee table?"

"Okay, okay, we get it," Brian said, and despite Jessica's desire to be entertained by his discomfort, she was a little embarrassed for him at this unexpected glimpse of *his* house.

But Michelle was not finished detailing how to spot a single person. "And what do you think her bathtub looks like?"

"I have no idea," he said tersely.

"I bet there's not a sooty ring around it."

"There's a sooty ring around my bathtub?" he asked, and

glared at Jessica as if she had discovered it and chastised him for it.

"Every time you tinker with that ugly old truck."

"My truck is not ugly," he said dangerously. "It's a classic. And to get back to the point, I didn't look in Jessica's oven, not that its contents could be taken as an indication of character. And I certainly didn't look in her bathtub."

Jessica's plan to remain detached seemed to be crumbling. In fact, she was finding these tiny glimpses into the personal life of Brian Kemp utterly fascinating.

But only, she defended herself fiercely, because she could feel satisfied he wasn't living nearly the life she would have thought. What would she have imagined? Ferraris, glamorous women, a whirlpool tub, no rings of soot or root beer. Maybe champagne.

"Well, if you did look in her oven," Michelle informed him, "there wouldn't be any dishes in it. Not like at your house."

"*Our* house," he corrected her.

"Whatever," she said with perfect indifference.

Jessica noticed how the indifference stung him. Why did he send a quick sidelong glance her way? Did he care what she thought about where he stored his dirty dishes? Why? When *her* character was under question? But apparently he did care because he gave his niece his sternest look.

"Michelle," he said, "having a conversation with you is like playing Ping-Pong with ten balls on the table at once. You seem to be deliberately missing the point, changing the subject and confusing the issue. It's not about bathtubs. I don't know Ms. Moran well enough to let you stay here. Not that you've been invited."

"Can't you tell everything you need to know by looking

around?" Michelle said. "You said yourself it looked like Snow White and the Seven Dwarfs could come singing out of the woods at any moment. This is not the home of some-one of questionable character!"

"You're going to be a lawyer," he groaned. "I just know it." Jessica noticed he sent another look her way. He was em-barrassed, not only by his lack of control over his niece, but also about the fact that he was familiar with fairy tales. Well, it was true that he did look like the man least likely to be fa-miliar with magical princesses.

Considering how much she had planned to relish his dis-comfort, she found her plan backfiring. She felt a little sorry for the man. Not much. Not enough to damage her resolve, just a thimbleful of pity.

"Even if Dopey or Snoozy or Sneezy or whatever comes forward with a character reference, *you have not been invited.* So…"

"A character reference?" Jessica repeated. He'd used up his thimbleful mighty fast. Of all the nerve! "May I remind you, you came here? Expecting a miracle? What kind of person wants a character reference from somebody they think can work miracles?"

She realized that, despite her vow to remain detached, she was feeling a passionate desire to pick up one of her garden shovels and clunk him over his handsome head.

"Nothing personal," he said, as if that would take the sting out of it. "My job makes me cynical."

"This is not the type of place an ax murderer lives," Michelle informed him. "I bet she gardens for a living. Right?"

Maybe a shovel murderer, Jessica thought. "I'm a horti-culturist."

"You don't know the first thing about murderers of any kind, Michelle," he responded, coolly.

"And you have the inside track 'cause why? Handing out speeding tickets and eating doughnuts has made you an expert?"

Brian went very quiet. Jessica could see the muscle working in his jaw again, and she knew instinctively he was counting to ten.

Michelle seemed to realize she had overplayed herself, but her confrontational tone softened only slightly. "Are you worried she might be growing a little hemp among the roses? Is that it? Are you going to shine your flashlight in her eyes and say, 'are your pupils dilated?'" She turned to Jessica. "He did that to me, you know."

Jessica knew that to give Michelle the sympathetic reaction she was looking for might be a mistake, but she let her annoyance at Brian cloud her judgement. "Really?" she said indignantly. "That's horrible."

Brian shot her a look that was not the least bit hard to interpret, and then he returned his attention to Michelle. Despite herself, Jessica was beginning to find his restraint admirable, which was unfortunate, since she really didn't want to find anything about him admirable.

"I said I was sorry I did that to you. Don't you let go of anything?" he asked.

Not if it could be used to her advantage, Jessica realized. She found this interchange very telling, but she was annoyed by her own less-than-stellar ability to detach. She was not sure how she could want to hit Brian on the head with a shovel and feel just a wee bit sorry for him at the same time, but she knew it was the kind of complication that spelled danger for her quiet little life.

Still, he just had it so wrong. Michelle wasn't the kind of girl who would unquestionably accept his authority. Had he been engaging in these power struggles with her for months? Had he won any?

"You knew Jessica in high school," Michelle pressed. "You said you saw her do a miracle. Jeez, you'd probably ask Moses for a character reference, even if you saw him part the Red Sea."

"I probably would," Brian said, without apology.

Michelle changed tactics with head-spinning swiftness. Suddenly, she smiled sweetly, touched her uncle's arm, blinked up at him.

"Please let me stay, Unkie. I won't be a nuisance. I'll help out. I'll sleep on the floor. I have to be with O'Henry. I have to."

Knowing it would be very unwise to take a side and knowing it would be even less wise to do anything that would put her in close proximity to Brian on a daily basis, Jessica still couldn't stop herself. Because, the argument aside, she had heard the very real need in Michelle's voice.

Jessica saw the truth, shining clearly, rising above all her confusion about Brian. The child needed to be with her dog.

And Jessica had to help the right thing happen. Yes, she had been hurt by life and hurt by love and some of that hurt could be attributed to this man in front of her. But had she let those hurts make her into the kind of a woman who could turn her back on what needed to be done for a wounded child?

Michelle was here, now, and so was the dog, and it was perfectly clear they both needed her. She couldn't turn her back on that, even if it would make her life so much easier and less complicated.

"Okay," she said. "Michelle can stay."

Brian turned and stared at her. That muscle in his jaw was really very attractive, probably because it worked so hard.

"Excuse me? I don't think that's your decision to make!" Despite his level tone, he was furious, his eyes snapping with anger.

"I think it would be a good idea for her to stay. I have an extra room." Jessica lifted her chin to meet his glare. She did not want or need this aggravating man's approval. Not by a long shot.

So, even if the look he gave her made her want to retract the invitation and run, she would not give him the satisfaction of having that kind of power over her. Instead, she smiled as sweetly at him as Michelle just had.

"Now, I've been invited!" Michelle crowed.

Brian glared at his niece and then at her. Jessica was very glad she was not on the wrong side of the law at the moment. She had a feeling he'd have her up against the wall and in cuffs in a heartbeat. She wondered if he would search her.

The thought, so naughty and so out of character, was a stern reminder of why she should not have done what she just did: tangle her life with his.

"Could I see you privately for a minute, Ms. Moran?" he said through clenched teeth.

Michelle rolled her eyes. "This is where he takes you aside and grills you. He did it to my friend Monica's mom before I could spend the night there. How embarrassing. 'Mrs. Lambert, are there weapons in your house? Do you use illegal drugs?'"

"How do you know that?" he snapped at his niece.

"Mrs. Lambert told me. She thought it was funny. And cute. But I didn't."

He'd obviously had enough of the exchange with his niece because he gave her a look so smoldering that it bought her sudden silence. Michelle could not hold his gaze and scuffed at the dirt in front of her with the toe of her sneaker.

Jessica felt his fingers bite into her elbow. She should have been insulted by his rough touch, but, unfortunately, it made her think more very naughty thoughts and made her highly aware of the threat he was to her well-ordered world. She was unceremoniously hustled out of Michelle's earshot.

He dropped his hold on her elbow, but it stung where he had touched, as though he had branded her with his anger. She found herself looking up into those chocolate-brown eyes. It felt like the years melted away, and she was sixteen all over again, her heart beating too fast, so filled with *wanting* that it hurt.

She reminded herself, firmly, that she had banished that girl who wanted things she could not have. Still, did he have to smell so good? So clean and purely masculine? Did he have to stand so close that she could count the lashes—thick and spiky—around his eyes?

His unsettling proximity made a dangerous question tease the corners of her mind. Could her adult self have what the younger version could not?

She was so different now. Slender. Confident. She might even go as far as to say pretty. Had she become the kind of woman who would stand a chance with him?

It was way too complicated a question. Wouldn't a relationship with him be a betrayal of who she was now, not to mention of who she used to be? Oh, sure, he was big and muscular and good-looking and smelled of some kind of heaven. But who was he? If he was still the insensitive, self-centered jerk he had once been, why would she want his attention? Why would she want to stand a chance with him?

For the pure fun of it, a renegade voice inside her whispered. *Come on, Jessica, wouldn't it be just a little bit fun to flirt with danger?*

Danger. That was what he represented to the sense of self she had developed over the past fourteen years. It felt like he could knock it all down with a wink, a smile, a kind word or a kiss.

She looked at his lips. "No!"

"Pardon?" he said.

She flushed, sure her cheeks would now match the color of her Agrippina China rose. "Uh, nothing. I was just thinking out loud."

"I hope about your answer to Michelle staying here."

It was true. Michelle had to go. To keep her here would be intertwining her life with that of this man who so obviously still wielded some kind of power over the part of her that wanted the things that made a woman weak and powerless: a man's smoldering lips, his hands, the touch of his skin beneath her fingertips, the dream of a soul mate.

And yet Jessica could not bring herself to retract her invitation to Michelle, even in the interest of her own self-preservation.

She had felt the neediness and loneliness radiating from that child, raw and painful. To turn her back on it would be like turning her back on her own younger self and on everything she believed.

Jessica's motto was *do no harm.* To turn away from Michelle's obvious need would be to do harm in a way she did not even fully understand.

"Your niece is welcome to stay," she said firmly. She folded her arms over her chest and tossed her curls. "I think she should."

His expression darkened, and his brows lowered. Unless she was mistaken, he was counting to ten again. She recognized the good in that. A certain animosity between her and Brian would be a defense against that ridiculous part of her that thought it would be fun to flirt with danger.

And he looked dangerous now, an angry light changing the landscape of his eyes to storm-tossed. The line around his mouth grew firm and hard, and he folded his arms over his chest. It made her own gesture seem silly. She doubted her movement had made her look the least bit massive or intimidating.

Of course, that was the point. He was trying to intimidate her. And it was working—not that she would ever let him see that. She tilted her chin a little more, gave her curls another careless toss.

But his voice, when he spoke, was hard and cold, the voice of a man too accustomed to giving orders and being listened to. Which of course only deepened her own determination not to see anything his way.

"Look," he said, "I don't think it's a good idea if I let her win on this one."

"Really?" Jessica said, and set her legs wide apart in a posture that mirrored his, exactly. "She looks to me like a kid who could use a few wins. If it's not too hard on your ego, that is."

"It's not about my ego," he said, every word bitten out.

"So, if it's not about you, should I assume it's about me? For some reason you've decided I can be trusted with a dog, but not with your niece, is that it? Was she right? Do you think I have a little hemp patch over by the compost?"

"That is not it! I don't remember you being difficult!"

"You spent less than two hours with me, fourteen years ago. You never gave me a chance to show if I could be difficult or not." But he remembered correctly. Oh, no, she had not been difficult. Not at all. She had been falling all over herself trying to get him to see *who* she really was. And for a mad moment, under the moon, she thought he had. She was certain of it. She had seen a light come on in his eyes, had seen him lean toward her, had felt his breath in her hair when he'd whispered, *I'll call.*

"Jessica, I didn't give you a chance because I was a dumb kid. I was superficial and self-centered, and I doubt if I'm much improved. But you'll be thrilled to know there is justice. Here you are surrounded by sweetness and flowers, and I'm picking up drunks and spending half my life in a car that smells like puke and, well, worse things.

"You know what else? Not one of those kids who thought the world revolved around them has what you have here."

"What do I have here?"

He hesitated. He looked around. His tone softened. "Michelle saw it. I can see it in your face. In this place. Some kind of peace."

Ha. Until half an hour ago!

"So, since I'm Mother Theresa's little sister," *though hopefully better looking,* "what is the problem with having Michelle stay?"

"I never forgot what you did for that dog that night, and I need you to help my niece keep her dog, if that's at all possible. And it's not that I don't trust you with her. Let me tell you, my job requires instant judgements of people. My life sometimes depends on whether I'm right or wrong. You have that look that is eminently trustworthy."

"What look is that?"

"Oh, you know. The kind of miffed librarian look."

"Really?" she said, and felt her lips pursing up just like a miffed librarian.

"Don't take it the wrong way. There aren't nearly enough people devoted to doing the right thing. Who are good. And kind. And gentle."

"Don't forget spunky," she said, since he was making her sound about as exciting as *A Child's Little Book of Prayers*.

"That remains to be seen."

Did it? That could be interpreted in the very same way as *I'll call* by someone with the least inclination for romance, which of course he had cured her of long ago. Thank goodness.

"I don't want her to stay here with you in case the damned dog dies," he said, his voice suddenly low, looking cautiously over Jessica's shoulder. "I don't think she can take much more."

Jessica sighed. It really wasn't about his ego. She could see the worry etched in his eyes.

Firmly, she said, "Brian, it's not up to you to decide how much she can take, or can't."

"It's my job now to protect her!"

The fierceness with which he said that actually made her feel the teeniest desire to be nice to him. Just for a few minutes. Until she got her way.

"There are some things that aren't even remotely in your job description," she told him. "Believe it or not, the sun rises and sets without your help. You seem to have a few control issues. They won't help you with Michelle."

"Better than hocus-pocus."

Her guard snapped firmly back into place. "That's what I do. Hocus-pocus. You knew it when you came here."

"A dog is different than my niece."

"Brian," she touched his arm, "you can't protect her from life, not unless you're prepared to lock her in a closet. Even then, a tree could fall through the roof."

"Hey, guess what? I already figured out I can't protect her. If I could, don't you think her mom and dad would still be here?"

"Leave her here," Jessica said. "We'll heal the dog, or we'll help him die. Either can be an incredible experience. Trust me. Just a little bit."

He looked at where her hand rested on his arm, and she went to move it away, but he laid his own hand over top of it. She could feel the leashed power in that hand, feel her own yearning.

"Okay," he said, his voice low and gruff.

"Okay," she said.

"Maybe she's better off out here," he conceded reluctantly. "I hate leaving her alone when I'm on night shift. She says she's too old for a baby-sitter."

"She is. She could be baby-sitting herself, for heaven's sake."

"Well, not for anyone who *liked* their baby."

"She does okay with the dog."

"Yeah, maybe it's just me that she's mean as a rattlesnake to."

"Probably."

"So," he said, "are there weapons in your house? Or illegal drugs?"

"I'm the miffed librarian, remember?"

He touched the side of her cheek with the palm of his hand. The gesture was unexpected and made her heart race anew. He studied her.

"That was a mistake. More like Tinker Bell, with fairy dust."

"Does that bring us back to the illegal drugs?" she asked, trying to hide the way his hand on her cheek made her feel. Feminine. Beautiful.

He seemed to realize he was touching her face, so he dropped his hand and then shoved it in his pocket. "I have this parenting book that I read under my covers with a flashlight and it says not to be afraid to ask. You know. About the drugs and weapons."

"Brian," she said taking pity on him, "it won't help you to be a cop around your niece. I understand that you care about her, and that's why you conduct these inquisitions before you let her do things, but even that crack about the baby-sitting shows you don't trust her judgement. Doesn't the book say anything about that?"

"I haven't got to that part yet. I'm not much of a reader." He shook his head sadly. "I had no idea she named the pup after a writer. I bought her the candy bar after she named him that. I didn't know why she didn't eat it."

Jessica felt a terrible stab of tenderness for him. He was trying so hard.

A shiver went up and down her spine, but she shied away from the thought that followed it. No, she owed him nothing. For the child and the dog she would do her best.

But Brian Kemp? Healing him was way out of her league.

Still, what could it hurt to offer an opinion?

"I just feel," Jessica said, choosing her words carefully, "you would make more headway with Michelle if you were able to tell her the truth."

"About?"

"The way you feel about her. Instead of grilling her friends and looking at her pupils with a flashlight you need to tell her you love her more than the earth, and that you're worried about her."

He actually flushed, a lovely shade of crimson that moved up his neck. "If I told Michelle that, she'd tell me to take a leap. And then she'd go dye her hair green and say, 'Do you still love me now?'"

"And wouldn't you say yes?"

"No. Okay. Maybe."

"Let her know you love her."

"She'll use it against me."

"You look like a big, strong guy. You can probably handle it," Jessica said dryly.

"You know, the truth is not always the best policy. For instance, when you do an interrogation, you always tell the bad guy that his friend spilled the beans, so he might as well give. It's generally a bald-faced lie, but sometimes it works. So, it's a lie but it accomplishes something good."

"Well, yes, maybe on the bad guys, which your niece isn't."

"She seems to think *I* am! You haven't been living with us for the last six months. She doesn't like me much."

Jessica reminded herself, firmly, that his healing was not her business. On the other hand, there would be places, and probably many of them, where his healing and Michelle's would be interwoven like threads in a tapestry.

"Look what happened the last time she loved," Jessica reminded him softly. "They died."

"Are you telling me she's scared of caring about me?" he asked, incredulous.

"Yes."

"She sure as hell doesn't act scared. What makes you think she's scared?"

Because I loved once, too. Oh, yes, it was a teenage love, more a fantasy than a reality, but that hurt made me afraid to give my heart again, too. How much worse must it be for Michelle?

"Good old hocus-pocus," she lied.

Chapter Three

It had been a hell of a night, Brian thought wearily as he drove home after his shift. A pair of drunks had taken him on, split his lip and given him a pretty good couple of punches to the ribs. The bruised flesh ached, and he was willing to bet it was ugly. Of course, after all the excitement, one of them could not resist puking in the back of his car.

After the paperwork, he'd gotten a break-and-enter call that had resulted in a foot chase. He'd run six city blocks, full out, until his heart felt like it was going to explode and his legs felt like they were turning to gelatin under a hot sun.

He'd gotten the perp, a young man at least half his age.

It was the kind of night that had once filled him with satisfaction—action-packed, a few bad guys off the streets, pitting his strength against all that was wrong out there and *winning*. But somehow, since the deaths of Kevin and Amanda, he questioned everything and nothing felt the same as it used to. He felt old. Last night after catching the young burglary suspect, all he could think was that he would have to spend the rest of his shift in a shirt encrusted with his own dried sweat.

The discontent had been there, vague and hovering around the edges of his mind. It had never been something strong enough for him to articulate. Until yesterday, blabbing his fool head off to Jessica about picking up drunks and driving around in a car that smelled like puke.

"Don't forget sweat," he muttered. "Maybe next time I see her."

To add to his general sense of discomfort, he had not seemed to be able to shake Jessica's words: *just tell her you love her more than the earth.*

It was that New Age sensitivity gibberish, of course, the type of thing he was terrible at and detested. Besides, his attempts to win over females—any age, any interest group— had always been colossal failures, starting with his mother. Kevin had been the golden child, who met her every expectation, including his choice of a career as a lawyer.

Brian had never been anything his mother wanted him to be. She wanted children who were quiet, obedient and respectful; he'd been loud, independent and rebellious. His unfortunate memory of his mother was of her face sucked in with disapproval every time he entered the room. He'd gone on to earn that very same look from most of the women he'd ever been with.

And then there had been the brief engagement to his high school sweetheart, Lucinda, but her reaction to his career as a cop had been identical to his mother's. Horror. Lucinda Potter was not marrying a *cop*.

And Michelle, after meeting the only woman he'd brought home since she'd moved in, a gorgeous blond personal fitness trainer, had rolled her eyes, and said, "Where on earth do you find someone like that?" He resented her insinuation that his failure in the companionship department might have something to do with his selection process. Anyway, that was the last time he'd been out. Four months ago now.

He'd decided women just didn't get it, or he didn't get them. You didn't decide a chat about the state of the relationship was imperative during the Super Bowl. You didn't tell a man you thought he should trade in a truck—one that had been faithful to him for more than a decade—for a brand-new car with a name he couldn't pronounce. Personally, if Brian never heard one more word about a broken fingernail or split ends, it wouldn't be soon enough.

But Brian had looked at Jessica's fingernails yesterday, on his way to looking for the wedding band or lack thereof, and she hadn't had any fingernails to speak of, broken or otherwise. And her hair had surely been too short to be split.

There was something about her eyes, a calmness that invited confidences, that made a man feel as if she could solve the mysteries of a restless heart.

"My heart is not restless," he said, and snorted with derision, just to prove it.

But when he pulled up in front of his house, moments later, it mirrored the way he felt. Empty. His house looked unlived in and uninviting.

It was a modest two-bedroom, stucco bungalow in a newer subdivision of Esquimalt. He kept the lawn mowed and the newspapers picked up, but this morning the house looked cold. He realized, embarrassed by such an unmanly thought, that it would be improved with some flowers, a little land-scaping.

Some of the neighbors had landscaped with twig trees sur-rounded by tiny shrubs.

He realized he yearned for something more flamboyant. Flowers mixed with grass falling all over each other. Since the look would be totally out of place in his well-ordered neighborhood, he supposed that was about *her*, too.

How could one visit have left him feeling so unsettled? As if he was suddenly seeing his life through Jessica's eyes?

There was an easy solution to that. Don't see her again. After all, it had worked last time. But even thinking that felt like a cheap shot.

He went around the side walk and in the back door. He had become accustomed to sharing mornings with Michelle as she got ready for school. She was perpetually grumpy, but better company than no one. More recently, the puppy had added some liveliness to the morning routine, particularly if some-body stepped in some pee.

He took off his boots, went up the four steps into his kitchen, and looked at his surroundings as if he was seeing them for the first time. The room was not messy, because he always shoved the dishes in the oven until he ran out, but it seemed suddenly lacking in any kind of personality.

Jessica's kitchen had not exactly been tidy. Why had it felt like it was brimming over with warmth and liveliness?

He had a plain, wooden kitchen set, its lines straight and clean and modern—Danish it was called. The fridge and stove gleamed white, and there were European-style cabinets as white as the fridge and stove. Venetian blinds, closed, covered the window over the sink. Now that it had been pointed out to him he found the odd little finger smudge, but it was still a nice room. Efficient. Roomy. Bright. But it needed *something*.

"Yeah," he said sarcastically, "like plants hanging from the ceiling and hundred-year-old chairs painted red and yellow."

A voice inside him did not pick up the sarcastic note. It said *exactly*.

There *she* was again, Jessica making her presence known in his life, even though she was thirty miles away. She was just a bit of a thing. How did she manage to exude so much power?

Hocus-pocus, he reminded himself. Well, he wasn't falling under her spell.

Okay, so his kitchen needed some color. Something over the window—a valance, he thought it was called—some cushions on the chairs, place mats on the table. That's why Sears had their whole-home plan, so guys like him could pick out some matching stuff without the complication of the little woman.

He stepped in the dog's water dish, something that was part of his morning routine, and wondered if he should get rid of it, just in case the dog did not return. *O'Henry* was painted on it in pink nail polish, the handwriting ridiculously curly, childish and feminine at the same time.

Had O'Henry made it through the night? The answering machine wasn't blinking, not that he was at all certain Michelle would call him to report a life tragedy. Brian glanced at the clock. Just now seven o'clock. Way too early for him to phone there.

Not that calling seemed like the right thing to do for a man who wanted to keep things tidy and impersonal. What was he going to say? Good morning? Did the dog die?

He wanted to hear *her* voice. Was Jessica casting a spell on him?

Annoyed with himself, he picked up the dish and emptied it, thought about it for a minute, and then tucked it into the cupboard under the sink, behind the garbage can, where it wouldn't be a reminder in case the dog was not coming home. He would not have been so sensitive a few months ago.

He looked at the clock again. He should sleep, but a different plan was formulating. If he showered, he could pick up some breakfast for all of them and be out there by eight-thirty. That seemed more diplomatic than phoning and asking if the dog had died.

He'd never been diplomatic before, he reminded himself sourly, but then Jessica was no busty, blond fitness trainer.

She would require more of him. Not that he was ever getting involved enough with her to care what she would require. But she did have his niece. She was working with the dog. She was doing him a favor. Would it hurt to be a nice guy?

Maybe.

Live dangerously. That had always been his motto. Besides, now that he knew a spell was being cast, he could guard against it. What was a little hocus-pocus in the face of the determination of an unmarried male to stay that way?

Did Jessica think of him that way? As a potential friend of the intimate variety? She had once. He had seen it in her eyes.

And he'd scorned her. So entertaining these kinds of notions about her was probably the most dangerous thing he'd done in years, and he chased criminals for a living.

Still, an hour later, with a box of doughnuts and three still steaming hot chocolates beside him on the bench of his truck, he pulled into the rose-scented drive.

It occurred to him, suddenly, that doughnuts were a bad choice. A terrible choice. Jeez. Jessica had been pudgy once. Bringing her a doughnut was probably akin to bringing a recovering alcoholic a bottle of rye whiskey.

Jessica and Michelle were out on the steps of the cottage when he pulled up, and for a moment he rested in the tranquility of the scene, both women with their faces turned to the sun, their hair radiant under its rays, the flowers opening all around them.

Michelle turned her head and actually smiled, as if happy to see him. She leaped to her feet and ran toward the truck as he got out. She was like a small girl, practically dancing. She had scrubbed off the makeup and had none to replace it.

Jessica had been right. Michelle might have the potential for great beauty. Which would mean boys. He'd have to fight them off.

"He's much better this morning," she said. "O'Henry's much better. His eyes are open. He licked my fingers!"

Brian had hoped much better meant frolicking around the yard, but he looked to the porch and saw that Jessica and his niece had had the dog nestled between them.

Jessica still sat on the porch. Her hair was damp from the shower, and it curled wildly around her face. Like his niece, she wore no makeup, and like his niece, her natural beauty shone through. She was wearing jeans the color of wheat, and she hugged one knee. Her feet were bare, which was a strange thing for him to find sexy, but he did. She had a man's white shirt on over an ivory camisole. It was a spell-casting outfit, if he had ever seen one.

"What happened to your face?" Michelle asked, suddenly, her smile fading.

"Nothing." He touched his lip. "A little scrap."

"Could you have been killed?" she asked angrily.

"No."

"Humph."

So much for the peaceful moment of earlier. She looked daggers at him, flung her hair over her shoulder, and marched back to the step. He decided he wouldn't have to fight off any boys after all. None of them would be able to brave a look like that.

He leaned back in the truck and retrieved the doughnuts and the tray of hot chocolate.

For someone who was casting a spell on him, Jessica did not look all that enthused to see him. Probably the doughnuts. She probably was thinking he was a total jerk. That was his track record *exactly*. Try to be a nice guy, yet come off as a total jerk.

Michelle lost no time in digging through the box until she found the one with the red jelly.

"I love red jelly," she told Jessica.

"That's nice of your uncle to remember." So, maybe she didn't think he was a total jerk after all.

"Humph," Michelle said, unimpressed by his sensitivity.

He sat beside her on the step, but she gave him an annoyed look and moved away, so he petted the dog. O'Henry opened his eyes and flapped his tail weakly. He tried to lift his head, but gave up and closed his eyes again.

Not hopeful, Brian thought, but did the dog seem minutely better? Some ease in his breathing that had not been there before?

"It's not exactly the breakfast of champions," he said, offering Jessica a doughnut. "I guess I should have brought something else."

Jessica looked at Michelle, who was now sporting a mustache of white icing sugar and sucking the red out of her doughnut. "It seems to me it's the perfect choice."

"Well, for her." Dumb thing to say. It was happening again. His curse was setting in. *Try to be nice and just see what happens, Kemp.*

"And for you?" she asked quietly. "What? Do you watch your weight?"

"Uh, not usually."

She got it, suddenly, and her eyes darkened with annoyance. "Oh, I get it."

"What?" Michelle asked innocently.

"Your uncle is concerned about me eating doughnuts," Jessica said, and took a big defiant chomp out of a chocolate éclair.

"You're not fat!" Michelle protested.

"No, not at all," he said quickly. "I mean you look great, Jessica. Gorgeous." He was bumbling around awkwardly, just as if he were under a spell. He gave her a suspicious look, but if she was casting spells it was of the toad-creating variety. Besides, he didn't need any help from her when it came to failure in the wooing department.

Not that he was wooing Jessica Moran! What a thought!

It occurred to him that he was bothered, just a little bit, that Jessica was not brewing a love potion for his benefit.

Women liked him. They had always liked him. Well, until they found out they couldn't interrupt the football game, that was.

But then again, Jessica was a bright girl, quite a bit brighter than some of his choices. She had learned her lesson.

Maybe she planned to teach him one. About unrequited feelings. But that would have to mean he had feelings for her. And he didn't. Okay, he liked her house and her garden and the color of her kitchen chairs. Okay, he liked the green of her eyes, and the way that camisole peeked out from under her shirt.

But those weren't *feelings*. Observations. Nearly clinical.

"I used to be heavy," Jessica told Michelle.

"Really? What happened?"

"I used to eat because I was unhappy. That's not a problem for me anymore." She gave him a haughty look that made it very clear he had been at least partially the source of her unhappiness.

"You were unhappy?" Michelle asked. "But why?"

Jessica had the power now to lower him even further in his niece's estimation, if that were possible, but for some reason she didn't.

"I just didn't fit in during my teens. I was an orphan. I lived with my aunt instead of my parents. I had different interests than the other kids."

"That's a little bit like me," Michelle said. "What kinds of different interests?"

"I liked flowers and herbs and experimenting with, um, things."

Magic, he added silently.

"I didn't like makeup, and I didn't have nice clothes. My aunt was poor, so I didn't get to many movies or own music. I never knew who any of the movie stars or rock stars were."

"You were a geek," Michelle pronounced, but with the affection of a kindred spirit.

"Definitely," Jessica admitted.

"And what about him? What was he like in high school?" Michelle turned and looked over at her uncle. He put on his best choir boy expression, hoping to influence Jessica's memory.

"He was the most popular boy in school," Jessica said, but

he could not help but notice her flat tone and the way she looked away.

"Well," Michelle said, and patted Jessica's leg, "there's no accounting for taste."

They both enjoyed a giggle at his expense.

"Hey," he said, and gave Michelle a little shove with his shoulder.

She shoved him back and returned her attention to Jessica. "Did you like him?"

Jessica didn't answer for a moment. "Sure," she said.

"Did he like you?"

"Didn't even know I was alive."

Michelle gave him a stern look. "Oh, no. Were you one of those, Unkie? Those awful boys who are so stuck-up and full of themselves?"

"Uh, I guess I was." She did not call him Unkie often, so she didn't completely despise him. Yet. If Jessica kept talking that could all change.

"There's a boy like that in my class," Michelle said, thankfully shifting the focus away from her uncle. "I said hi to him once, and he just looked right through me, like I was a bug or something. I hate him."

Brian was surprised to find he did, too. Just like that. Wanted to rip some strange boy limb from limb because he had dared to hurt his niece. See? He'd been absolutely right yesterday. Life provided justice, extracted revenge.

"Did you know my mom?" Michelle asked Jessica.

"Not very well," Jessica said, and Brian noticed how careful her tone was.

"What was she like? From the little bit you did know her?" Michelle asked.

Brian closed his eyes. *Mean as a rattlesnake* would be an accurate description, but Jessica was, thankfully, way too wise to say it.

"I didn't know her, Michelle. I knew who she was, from a distance. She was very, very beautiful. All the boys liked her. She was always the center of attention."

Michelle contemplated that, then sighed. "She was really, really nice. The best mom in the whole world."

Brian opened his eyes and looked closely at his niece. Okay, Kevin and Amanda had moved to Toronto shortly before Amanda was born, and he certainly didn't know the intimate details of their family life.

But Amanda the best mom in the whole world? Not unless she'd had a brain and heart transplant.

He'd gone to see them every year at Christmas. Amanda had seemed resentful of her small daughter's many needs. Not to mention way too fond of afternoon cocktails.

He saw Jessica's eyes resting on his face and he felt transparent under her probing gaze. He finished his hot chocolate and thought of leaving. He didn't want to.

"I should go," he said, nonetheless.

To his vexation, nobody argued.

"Could you bring me some clothes?" Michelle asked. "My overalls. A T-shirt. My white shorts. Oh, and some undies."

He could feel his face getting red. *Undies*? Get real. "How long are you planning on staying, anyway?"

"Just until O'Henry is better," she said, way too fast. Her eyes said something different. They said *forever*.

In one day Jessica had succeeded in doing what he had been trying to do for six months. She had won his niece over. But try as he might to work up some resentment over that, he couldn't.

Michelle looked different. Even with her dog near death beside her. Even with him having committed the sin of getting his lip split at work, she looked different. Not quite content, but not so hard and hostile, either.

Of course, there was no war paint on her face this morning. Maybe that was all it was.

"Is that okay with you?" he asked Jessica.

She nodded. "She's a great kid. And she beat me at Scrabble twice in a row last night. I've been looking for some competition for so long. I'm addicted."

"To Scrabble?" he said, and laughed.

She suddenly flushed scarlet, realizing exactly what an addiction to Scrabble told him about her life. "That must sound very boring to you," she said stiffly.

But it didn't. It sounded, well, solid somehow. Wholesome. Michelle adored Scrabble, and she must love being with someone who knew how to play it, and who actually didn't mind losing.

He'd played Monopoly with his niece twice. He was competitive as hell and hated losing. He suddenly saw very clearly why she said *no thanks* whenever he brought out any game.

Michelle needed to be here, more than she needed to be with him. He hated admitting that, it was part of that competitive spirit. But wasn't being competitive about proving you were good enough? And wasn't that what his life had become? He wanted to be good enough for his niece. Good enough to make her whole and happy.

And he obviously was not.

"I'll give you a couple of bucks," he said, and could hear the gravel of emotion he was trying to suppress in his voice.

Jessica looked insulted. "She's no problem."

"Yeah," Michelle said.

That wasn't the message he'd been trying to give—that Michelle was a problem. Really, women and men belonged on separate planets. How much more peaceful that would be.

And lonely.

"Can I bring you anything, then?"

"Like more doughnuts?" Jessica asked sweetly.

It was a trick question, he knew it. "If that's what you want," he said.

She actually laughed, and he knew he had passed somehow. "No more doughnuts." She hesitated. "If you really want to do something for me, I'm trying to build a pond."

"Be glad to help," he said, and he found that he meant it. He told himself he was just repaying her for taking in his niece and the dog.

But it was more. He didn't really want to live on a different planet. Maybe if he hung out here, on the fringes, he could learn to speak their language.

"I'll come back tomorrow. Michelle, can you last that long without the clothes?"

"If I have to," she grumbled.

"Okay. See you tomorrow." He got up off the step, hoping one of them would ask him to stay and have another doughnut. Maybe he could even learn to play Scrabble.

"Wait."

Now they had the idea. But Jessica left him standing there while she got up and went in the house. She came back with two small jars. She opened one and touched his swollen lip with her fingertip. "This is for your lip."

Her fingertip, gentle as the touch of a butterfly wing, took his breath away.

Whatever she put on his lip felt thick and slippery. It was like ice, and it grew colder. It felt like his lip was burning, it was so cold. And then abruptly the sensation stopped, and there was no pain at all.

"This one," she folded his hand around the other jar, "is for your bruise."

"What bruise?" Michelle asked suspiciously.

"Yeah," he challenged her, "what bruise?"

She rested her hand on his side, right below his rib cage. Her touch was exquisite—fire and rain. Still, he flinched. "That one," she said.

"I don't know how much of this hocus-pocus I can handle," he groused, and turned quickly away before she could see the hidden confusion that he felt as clearly as she had seen that hidden bruise.

"Don't get the jars mixed up," Jessica called after him.

"Or what?"

"You'll turn into a toad."

Jessica and Michelle cackled happily, and he felt strangely left out of the circle of their warmth.

It wasn't hocus-pocus at all, of course. Jessica had noticed he was moving stiffly. He had sat down carefully when he joined them on the steps. His lip had been split on the right side. So, if he'd been two punched, a left and a right, she deduced that it was his left side that got the other punch. So much of what people thought of as magic was just keen observation, noticing the smallest details and listening for the small whisper of inspiration.

If she really had any kind of power, Jessica thought, she'd do well to use it on herself. Poof. A little restraint, please.

If you really want to do something for me, I'm building a pond.

How she would like to snatch those words back! As if she needed Brian Kemp to help her build a pond! That was not the message that she wanted to give him about her life. She did not need anyone!

She was quite capable of building a pond herself. Of course, she had been dreaming about it for years and hadn't quite figured out all the ins and outs, yet, but that didn't mean she *needed*.

"Want another doughnut?" Michelle asked, watching her uncle drive away.

"Of course," she said.

"Does that mean you're unhappy?" Michelle giggled.

With myself. The problem was he was so rotten good-looking, so ruggedly charming, that a woman was begging him to build ponds before she even knew it.

Not to mention reaching up to put balm on his lip. Touching his lip had been a mistake. It looked hard, but it wasn't. His lip had been soft as the inside of a rose petal. Jessica shivered remembering it and felt a terrible weakness at her core. *Wanting.*

She had the awful sinking sensation that maybe Brian was the one working the hocus-pocus on her. Just like last time.

"Are you having another doughnut?" Michelle asked, impressed. "That makes three. You must be *very* unhappy." And then she giggled again.

The dog managed to raise his head at the sound of her happiness. He adjusted himself minutely, laid his head on her lap, and sighed.

"Have you ever noticed," Jessica asked her, touching the

silkiness of the dog's ears, "that just when your life is exactly as you want it, you get thrown a curveball?"

"Have I ever!" Michelle agreed vehemently.

Chapter Four

Early the next morning, Jessica sat on the steps of her porch and watched the early morning sun paint her gardens in gold.

Michelle, an impossibly early riser, was already dressed and in one of the flower beds, planting seeds Jessica had given her yesterday. The girl's face, lit by those same golden rays, was dirt-smudged. She looked remarkably young. The puppy, doing somewhat better this morning, made several drunken efforts to help his mistress by digging beside her, then finally collapsed right on top of her toes. Michelle grinned down at him, tousled his ears and kissed his nose.

Happiness. It snuggled around Jessica like the warm, scented earth that she had dug her bare toes into.

Jessica did not consider herself wise, or sage, but she had grasped a remarkable life lesson: genuine happiness often caught her by surprise. And those unexpected moments rarely occurred in the places that promised them, like amusement parks or shopping malls or fancy restaurants.

No, those moments seemed to be borne in on the fragile butterfly wings of simplicity and silence. When Jessica would become aware of the slant of light, the scent of a rose, the look of innocence on a child's face, her heart would feel remarkably full.

But this morning's moment of tranquility was shattered when in the distance she heard the sound of Brian's truck turning into her drive. It seemed ridiculous that she would recognize, already, the low growl of that powerful engine, but she did. And it reminded her of the other thing she knew about happiness, it could be fleeting.

Because, at the sound of that truck drawing nearer, her moment of contentment was instantly replaced with anxiety.

Have you ever noticed, she had said to Michelle yesterday, *that just when your life is exactly as you wanted, life throws you a curveball?*

Brian Kemp was her curveball. Jessica had not expected him to arrive so early. How did she look? Awful, of course. Her hair did not like to be tamed at the best of times, in the early morning it scattered around her head in a wild disarray of rebellious curls.

She had not dressed, just grabbed a coffee and come out onto the steps. Now she was aware her plaid pajama bottoms were too large and not the least sexy, especially given the fact she had coupled them with a T-shirt that read Gardeners Have Great Bloomers.

Annoyed with herself for even thinking of trying to impress him by changing, she planted herself even more firmly on the step.

She was thirty-one years old, far too old to be feeling so girlishly anxious about the arrival of a man, even if he was a dreamboat.

Dreamboat. That was the whole problem. Brian's unexpected arrival in her life had lurched her backward in time. He was forcing her to revisit a past fraught with insecurities.

That was the only rational explanation for why she was rehearsing snappy greetings in her head, all designed to convince him that she was not the type of woman who would ever spend a single moment of her life rehearsing snappy greetings.

He pulled up in a shower of gravel and dust, his truck careening to a halt.

"Yeah," Jessica muttered to herself, "he moves too fast. And if he's like that with his truck, he's like that with everything."

Then, without him having said one single word, she felt herself blushing. And rehearsing how to reject him if he had the audacity to try any fast moves on her.

He leaped out of the truck, rummaged around in the bed of it, and then came toward her, loaded down with a shovel and a crate.

She lifted her hand in what she could only hope was not too enthusiastic a greeting. She ordered herself to look back to her moment of happiness, the child and the dog busy in the garden. But her mind mutinously refused, choosing the more dangerous picture.

For he *was* a danger to her, and it was never more apparent than now as she watched him saunter down the walk. His dark hair fell charmingly over one eye, his near-white jeans with the hole in the knee hung loose from sensuous hips. His arms had lovely bulges and ripples in all the right places, and his chest was full and deep beneath a navy blue police T-shirt.

"Mornin'," he said, setting the crate beside her, and throwing himself onto the step below her. She moved her feet just before he landed on them and tried to curl her now-dirty toes under the step.

"I hope that's not doughnuts," she said, eying the crate warily, her snappy greetings completely wiped from her mind by the delicious scent that tickled her nostrils.

Not doughnuts.

Man smell. Clean and crisp, intoxicatingly masculine. A smell that invited a woman to lean a little closer, inhale a little deeper. A smell that could melt a well-rehearsed rejection before it had a chance to fully mature.

He laughed. His teeth flashed white in the sun, and the brown of his eyes twinkled with sparks of merriment. "Something better."

The only thing she knew of that was better than doughnuts was Belgian chocolate, and if that crate was full of that, she might as well just head for the Big-as-a-Barge section of ladies' wear, not for the first time in her life. Odd, that being huge could render one invisible, especially to a man like him. Though considering how tongue-tied and gauche Jessica felt at this moment, invisible didn't sound half bad.

"Ta-da."

He pulled something out of the box. The object was a mystery to her: metal caked in grease and grime. If she had to guess, she would say it was a lawn mower engine, though the thick and somewhat frayed electrical cord that dangled from the apparatus made her pretty sure that was not it.

It was definitely the type of slightly-repulsive object only a man would consider better than a doughnut.

"Look what I found," he said with the kind of affection that would make any red-blooded woman envious. "It was going to get thrown out."

He scowled at this. Obviously throwing out such prizes was something he would have liked to see made an indictable offense.

"Um. What is it?" For a man who worked fast, this seemed to be an indirect route to making the move on her. She wanted him to get on with it, so she could squash him like a bug.

She wanted him to make the move on her because she wanted him—needed him—to find her attractive. *Oh, Jessica,* she said to herself, *if you had an ounce of sense you would get rid of this man, fast.*

"A pump," he said happily. "For our pond."

Our pond. The statement was casually thrown out. The phrasing made her feel quite giddy, a reminder that her life was linked with his, whether she liked it or not.

And oh, she liked it. She liked having this vibrant, impossibly good-looking man sitting on her front porch pulling ugly items out of boxes. She liked the way the sun spun his hair to silk and the flash of his smile. She liked the ripple of the muscle in his arms and the way his knee, square and covered in springy hair, popped out through the threaded hole in his jeans.

She liked it, and hated herself for liking it. Vulnerability did not sit well with her. A reminder that, if she didn't want to get hurt all over again, she had to send Brian Kemp packing. If she had an opportunity to squash his ego like a bug before she got rid of him, so much the better.

But before she could correct him—it was not in any way, shape or form, *their* pond; it was *her* pond—his attention was diverted.

"Good grief, is that Michelle?"

Before she could answer he was off the step and moving toward the garden.

The behind of those jeans was nearly as threadbare as the knee. She felt her dignity evaporating. If she didn't get herself under control, she was going to be the one putting the moves on him! Considering her lack of expertise in this area, she would be leaving herself wide-open to, well, getting squashed like a bug.

"Hey kid, I didn't know you ever got up before the crack of noon."

Jessica watched as Michelle turned to her uncle and caught the brief shining welcome in her eyes before it was quickly masked.

"Well, that's because there's something to do *here*," she said defensively.

"You can't stick seeds in a patch of dirt anywhere?" Brian asked, earning himself a roll of the eyes. Jessica wished she hadn't seen his quick wince of pain before he diverted his niece's attention from his own failings by saying, "Hey, look at O'Henry."

At the mention of his name, the pup lurched gamely to his feet and gamboled across the short distance between Brian and his niece before collapsing at Brian's feet.

He got down unhesitatingly, rolled the dog over, scratched the matted hair on its tummy as the pup waved his paws ecstatically at the sky.

Jessica felt her own vulnerability again as she saw the big

man practice such exquisite gentleness. Of course, it was gentleness she had seen in him a long time ago, too, as he had bent over another dog, his face pained, but his hands tender.

She shook off the vision.

"Did he bring doughnuts?" Michelle called eagerly.

"Something better," Jessica called back, and watched as Michelle brushed off her knees and came bounding toward the steps. The puppy pushed away from Brian and tottered after her.

"What's better than doughnuts?" Michelle asked. "Chocolate?"

"A woman after my own heart," Jessica said, and pulled back the flap on the carton so Michelle could look inside. The girl shook her head. "Men," she said with disgust.

"My sentiments exactly," Jessica said.

"Hey, I rescued that pump from the dump."

Now, this was a statement only a fool would think of as romantic, and yet the thought of him rescuing a pump for *her* pond made Jessica feel frighteningly soft inside.

She had to fight this feeling!

"And," he reached over and ruffled his niece's hair, "the doughnuts are on the front seat of the truck. Red jelly. So, now am I your hero?"

"Okay," Michelle said. "For five minutes. Don't let it go to your head." She softened her remark with a smile and flounced over to the truck.

The look in his eyes could have melted chocolate, and Jessica felt again, piercingly, her vulnerability. *Get rid of him.*

"Look, Brian, when I mentioned *my* pond, I wasn't picturing anything complicated. A little dip in the ground with some water in it where I can float a few water lilies. That's all. It would take an hour of your time. Maybe two at the out-side. " He looked aghast, and so she added, a little less firmly than she might have liked. "Really."

"Even the most rudimentary pond needs a pump," he ex-plained to her carefully, as if she were an idiot child who had refused a gift from Santa Claus. "Standing water becomes a breeding ground for mosquitoes. And lovely green slimy stuff."

"Oh," she said weakly. "Green slimy stuff."

"How do you know so much about ponds?" Michelle asked, bringing back the doughnuts and plopping herself con-tentedly on the steps. "Arrest a pond burglar last night?" She chortled at her own mean wit.

"I read about it!" he said.

"You read?" Michelle asked incredulously. "You don't even take the newspaper."

"Just because I choose not to read, doesn't mean I don't know how," he said with grave dignity.

"When did you read about it?" Michelle pressed.

He looked embarrassed. He slid Jessica a look. "Last night," he said.

But Jessica felt the same about his sudden interest in read-ing about ponds as she had about him finding a discarded pump. It was for her, somehow, and it made her feel cared about in ways she did not want to feel from Brian Kemp.

Michelle eyed her uncle narrowly. Then she slid Jessica a look, and then looked back at her uncle.

"Are you trying to impress Jessica?" she asked bluntly.

Jessica could feel her face suffuse with heat. She took a sudden interest in burying her toes deeper beneath the stairs. She hazarded a glance at Brian.

His face was the color of a brick.

"No!" he said, too quickly. "I'm not trying to impress anyone. I'm just paying her back. For having you."

"Oh, I get it, like I'm such a burden," Michelle snapped.

"I meant for helping with O'Henry, too," he said, but it was too late and with one last searing glance Michelle gathered up her doughnut and the remainder of the box, and stomped back to her flower bed, her dog waddling drunkenly behind her.

The silence was thick. Jessica wanted to look anywhere but at the hurt in his eyes. Or at her own wound.

She had thought it was about her.

But it wasn't. It was about owing. That was so much better, wasn't it? So why did she feel bruised?

It was a warning, that was all. A warning not to get romantic notions about this man, not to read too much into anything he said or did.

I'll call, after all, had meant sometime in the next twenty-five years.

"Jeez," he said finally, "how do I always manage to get it so wrong? Every single time?"

"It's a gift," Jessica said, resisting the urge to comfort him.

He snorted. "That's true. My gift. Or my curse, depending how you look at it." His eyes narrowed on the letters on her T-shirt and she folded her arms firmly over her chest, ignoring the tiny ripple of sensation she felt at the unexpected heat in his eyes.

"I brought the books for you to look at," he said and pulled his eyes, thankfully, away from the message on her T-shirt and refocused on the box. He pulled out several manuals, magazines and plan books, all now splotched with grease from the pump.

The man had no idea how to treat a book, Jessica thought, looking for things to dislike about him, no matter how flimsy.

"This was my favorite," he said, opening a page and handing it to her.

She stared at it. Her defenses wavered. *Owing* would be about building the simple little oval pond on the facing page—a shallow dip, just as she had described—that she could fill with water and float a few water lilies in.

But this.

It was an enchantment. The pond, constructed exquisitely from rock, looked as if it had been stumbled across in a forest glade. It was actually two ponds, tiered, one above the other. A small pond, delightfully natural looking, formed the upper portion. A waterfall overflowed from it, dropping water a foot or so into the second larger pond.

"This is way more than I had in mind," she forced herself to say. "Way more. No. This other one is fine."

That complicated pond would keep him in her life for how long? Days? Weeks? The other, simpler project would probably only take a few hours.

"I know which one you want," he said, "it's written all over your face."

So, she was that transparent to him. Perhaps it had been written all over her face all morning how much she would have liked to smooth his hair beneath her fingertips, touch that lively muscle in his upper arm.

Taste his lips.

"I have to go," she said. "Shower. Breakfast. You know." She couldn't get her transparent face away from him fast enough.

"I know," he said, softly, as if he really did, as if he knew each treacherous thought that had flitted through her brain since he appeared on her doorstep.

She got to her feet and hurriedly made her way up the stairs, opened the door, felt the cool of her cottage offering her safety and security. The life she had made for herself beckoned, promising her sanctuary.

"Hey," he said, before she shut the door on him.

If he asked her to stay outside on the step with him and eat doughnuts she would. The awful truth was, she would stay with him even if he only invited her to inspect the other grease-encased treasures he had squirreled away inside that crate.

What had happened to the strong woman who was going to get rid of him? Who was going to reject his effort to put the move on her? Simple. When he hadn't, she had become a desperate woman.

"Yes?" she said with all the prim dignity of the old spinster that she was.

"I didn't get to see your bloomers yet."

She stared at him, speechless.

"Well, you're the one advertising. On your T-shirt. Bikinis?" he guessed hopefully.

She was unprepared for the charm of his teasing, or for how flustered it made her feel. Was this kind of like making a move on her? It was a terribly suggestive topic for a short acquaintance, even if the T-shirt had invited it.

A gentleman would have ignored the T-shirt. But the pirate-like twinkle in his eyes reminded her he was no gentleman.

But his guess was so wrong. Bikinis? Ha. Plain, sensible white cotton of no particular style, though she seemed to recall cruel girls in the gym change room at high school referring to them as "mommy-bought." She slammed the door so hard the glass rattled in the frame.

There. How was that for rejection?

But the door was not thick enough to keep his voice from sliding over her.

"A gift," he said with sad, but slightly insincere, remorse.

Ah, yes he did seem to have a gift for making the women he cared about the most furious with him. And he didn't have to half-try to do it.

Not that Jessica would fit into that category. A woman he cared about.

He hardly knew her. Only that wasn't quite right. He felt like he knew her. He felt like the tilt of her chin told him how proud and fierce she was, and the light in her eyes how soft and vulnerable. The too large clothes told him she was shy, and the sensuous curve of her full lips told him that a single kiss would take her beyond shy in a twinkle.

She had made an absolutely delightful sight this morning, her elfin face framed by curls gone askew. Her too baggy pajamas swam around her slight frame, hinting at subtle but delectable curves underneath. Her ankles had been bare and slender, her feet coated with a fine film of dust. It was ludicrous, given the number of outfits designed to entice, that the sight of those ankles had stirred him.

What did that shirt say? Gardeners Have Great Bloomers.

That's exactly what she looked like. The kind of gal who would wear bloomers. Old-fashioned somehow. Prim. Proper. But just underneath that, did passion burn, hot and ripe? Had she run from herself or from him just now?

Well, she needn't worry. Jessica Moran was not his kind

of gal at all. He'd become accustomed to a more hard-bitten kind of woman. One who looked wistful over diamonds. Who would not blush at the mention of bloomers. Who would play the flirt-and-parry game with ease and enjoyment, not with self-consciousness.

Which probably explained his lack of any kind of love life for a number of years. It was all too predictable. It made him tired before it began. There was something vaguely and disturbingly plastic about his relationships thus far.

Jessica was something different. She was real. Genuine. It was refreshing. Enchanting, actually.

And he recalled, now, that he'd seen a glimpse of that all those years ago, and he'd been drawn to it then, too. Had he sensed in her, then, that she might be the one who could lead him away from what his life was becoming? That she could take him from a superficial world to a deeper place?

Oh, he'd sensed it all right. Jessica was a woman, then and now, who would require a man to be more than he had ever been before. He'd done the sensible thing, way back when, which was to run like hell.

Because no matter how refreshing she was, she'd still be insulted if he chose a football game over her.

So, he'd do the sensible thing this time, too. Once he'd cleared his debt. Because he owed her. He owed her for a phone call he'd never made. He owed her for the happiness being coaxed to bloom in his niece's eyes. He owed her for the puppy who, he allowed himself to hope for the first time, was going to make it.

So, she was going to get the pond of her dreams. And then he'd gather up his niece and his dog and his tools and be gone from her life. It was that simple.

Somewhere, he heard water turn on. He tilted his head and pinpointed the tiny window where the sound came from. The lace curtains flitted out of the window and back in, dancing with the breeze.

She was showering. The picture that suddenly crowded his mind made his mouth go dry. And he wondered if anything was going to be as simple as he wanted it to be.

Brian heaved himself up off the steps, scooping up his shovel and his crate. He stopped where Michelle was working and snagged a doughnut.

She ignored him.

"I didn't mean to insult you," he said after a minute. "I just meant she's feeding you, and keeping you, and she doesn't look like she can really afford it."

"I had no idea I was so expensive," Michelle said haughtily.

"Michelle, what I'm trying to say is that when people do me a kindness I try to do one back."

"So, now its a kindness that I've been taken off your hands."

It was on the tip of his tongue to say what he always said. Why did she have to twist everything he said? Why did everything have to turn into a battle? Then he remembered Jessica's words.

Tell her the truth.

He touched her shoulder. "Sweetie, you are no burden to me. I love you very much. I would do anything in my power to change the circumstances that brought you to me, but not the fact that you are with me."

Michelle rocked back on her heels and stared at him, stunned. "Humph," she said, turning rapidly back to her planting. But not before he had seen that, somehow, he had finally said the right thing.

He looked around the garden, recognized the magic in this place, and shook his head in wonder and bafflement.

Now he *really* owed Jessica.

A week later, he was wishing he'd picked the smaller pond. It had been a long time since he'd held a shovel. A long time since he had pitted his brawn against the earth. The ponds were moving very slowly, since he could only spare an hour or two a day. It was a bigger task than he'd envisioned. And yet, for all that, he felt good, too. Breathing hard, working, sweat trickling in his eyes. Too busy to give any more thought to naked woodland nymphs in the shower.

He stopped to look around and saw Jessica coming across the lawn with a pitcher of what looked to be lemonade and three glasses.

She had changed over the past week. Was she making an effort to look more attractive? Was it for him? Or was it just that as he got to know her better, she seemed more beautiful? The woman was a constant challenge, of course, but she was also funny and smart, and he found himself looking forward to their verbal jousting.

He'd rather expected one of those sessions when he'd called yesterday. "Jessica, I can't make it tonight. Me and a couple of the guys are watching football at El Toro's."

He'd expected her to remind him that he'd committed, to tell him his niece needed to see him daily, to be annoyed.

"Great," she'd said. "Michelle and I want to go see a movie tonight, anyway."

"What movie?"

"The Heart's Way Home."

He waited for her to ask if maybe he would like to come

to the movie instead of watching the game. When she said nothing, he heard himself saying, "If I was a nice guy, I'd probably come to the movie instead of watching football."

Jessica had actually laughed out loud. "You'd *hate* this movie. Michelle and I will enjoy it much more without you groaning at all the good parts and rustling about restlessly."

"Well, have fun," he said.

"You, too," she said and sounded like she meant it. Of course, he hadn't had any fun at all. The teams had been mismatched and the final score was dismal. His mind kept drifting, wondering what the heck Jessica thought the *good* parts would be.

Today, she was wearing a little sundress and a straw hat. The straps were slender on her shoulders, and she looked exquisitely feminine. The sun poured through her dress, outlining the slender length of her legs.

Michelle materialized beside him. "She's awfully pretty," she said innocently.

"Uh-huh."

"And really nice."

"Uh-huh."

"I think you should ask her out on a date."

He was lucky the lemonade had not arrived, because he would have choked on it. He decided he liked it better when Michelle didn't like him.

"She's not my type," he said gruffly.

"Well, if she's not, you're stupid."

There, that was more like it.

"Hi," Jessica said. "I brought out some lemonade. You guys seem bushed." She looked from face to face. "What?"

"Nothing," Brian said.

"I was just saying to Unkie…"

"Here," he said, grabbing a cup off the tray, "have some lemonade." He thrust the cup into Michelle's hands and in his eagerness to shut her up, upset the whole tray. It capsized, in what seemed to be slow motion but not slow enough for him to catch it. The contents spilled all down the front of Jessica's dress.

Making it very clear to him that Jessica was not wearing any bloomers at all.

He had taken off his shirt earlier. He grabbed it and made a valiant effort to blot her off. He could feel the lovely resilience of her slender frame beneath his clumsy efforts, and he went very still.

She wrestled the shirt from him. "Stop it," she said. "I'm perfectly fine, I'll do it myself. Here, I'll get some more lemonade. And change."

She bent over to pick up the toppled pitcher. It wasn't only bloomers she wasn't wearing. She was an astounding woman. Soft. Firm.

His breath was coming in tight little gasps.

"Michelle was just saying I should ask you out on a date," he was amazed to hear himself saying.

She straightened abruptly and glared at him with a kittenish fury that he knew would be a terrible mistake to find amusing.

"*Michelle* thought you should ask me on a date," Jessica repeated flatly, juggling the tray and empty pitcher so that she covered the best of her wet spots.

"Well, not really. I mean, I would have thought of it, too, eventually."

"Really?" She did not sound pleased, or flattered. The old Jessica would have knocked him over in her delight.

"Yeah. So what do you think?" He knew this was going badly. He could not believe how, at his advanced age, his hormones had just totally overruled his brain.

So, he should have been relieved with her answer.

She leaned close to him. Her wet dress actually touched his bare chest. She smiled sweetly. And said, "Not if you were the last man on earth."

He expected Michelle to guffaw. Instead she was giving him a look of abject disappointment.

"It's a gift," he muttered in way of explanation, then turned his back on them both and put some muscle into the dummy end of that shovel.

He allowed the sting of those words to gnaw at him the rest of the afternoon. Not if you were the last man on earth. From Jessica. Jeez.

When the hole for the pond was just about down to China his niece sidled over.

"Unkie," she said, glancing around discreetly to make sure she was not overheard, "you're a little rusty in the romance department."

He gave her a blistering look, which she ignored.

She smiled sweetly. "So, I've decided to help."

"Oh, great."

"I'm going to be your personal romance coach."

It was on the tip of his tongue to yell that the last thing on earth he wanted was a romance. Especially with Jessica. And wasn't that a fun coincidence, because she wouldn't go out with him if he was the last person on earth, anyway.

But something in his niece's face stopped him from uttering the sharp words.

Her eyes were glowing with a light that he had given up

ever seeing. In fact, after a week of working with Jessica in the garden she looked fresh. Her face was clearing up. She looked like she might be gaining a bit of weight. She wasn't wearing black all the time.

But the best thing was that his niece actually had hope. It shone in eyes that had been dull for way too long. Michelle had a sudden inkling that maybe the world could be a fun place, a place where the unexpected twists and turns were not all bad ones. His niece wanted to believe in fairy tales and in love and in miracles.

Was that such a bad thing?

Chapter Five

Brian realized that he had to think rationally, long term not short term. He wanted to encourage that bright light of hope that he saw dancing in her eyes for the first time in recent memory.

But for the long term, he had to think of exactly what it was she was hoping for. Looking at Michelle, he became uneasily aware this was not about him and Jessica going on a date. Oh, no, in her fevered teenage mind she would be looking for far more than that.

Happy endings, of course.

Even if, God forbid, he ever took the snooty, bloomer-free Ms. Moran on a date, he certainly wasn't looking for happily-ever-after. His niece would end up more destroyed than ever when her juvenile romantic notions were crushed. And he somehow doubted whether Jessica would appreciate being used to glue his niece's psyche back together.

Still, it would be intriguing to explore the depths of Jessica's green-gold eyes, to see what it was like to make her laugh helplessly, to touch that place on her cheeks where the freckles...

Stop, he ordered himself. Intrigue aside, he could not take Jessica on a date because Michelle wanted him to.

Having come to his senses, he said, "You heard the lady. She wouldn't go out with me if I was the last man on earth."

"Oh, she didn't mean that. You just hurt her feelings."

He didn't like the idea that he had hurt Jessica's feelings, but it was no big surprise. Despite the fact that she had spent a week ignoring him, even from a distance he could not miss Jessica's softness. She was vulnerable. And he was a man with a gift, a documented talent for being a bull in the china shop of feelings.

Michelle studied his face, and he knew she had decided to capitalize on the remorse he had not been quick enough to hide.

"That's the part I could help you with," she offered eagerly. "Being more sensitive. Women like sensitivity."

"You're going to teach me about sensitivity?" he said. Michelle had criticized everything in his life from his job to his haircut to the contents of his fridge. She had stomped on his every effort to make her feel at home in his home!

She nodded, absurdly eager to get her juvenile hands on his private life. Sheesh. Sensitivity lessons from Attila the Hun would probably be more productive, though he refrained—just barely—from saying so. Instead, he used his most measured, mature-uncle-to-impressionable-young-girl voice.

"Michelle, no. Banish the thought. I do not need sensitivity training. I do not want to be sensitive. I do not want to be around the kind of woman who requires sensitivity."

"That explains Bambi, the fitness trainer."

"Her name wasn't Bambi."

"What was it, then?"

He couldn't remember. Tiffany, maybe. "She was four months ago, and there is a reason for that. I do not want a date. If I did want to date, you would not see nearly as much of me as you do on Friday and Saturday nights."

Could he be any clearer? Apparently he had to be, because Michelle was opening her mouth, prepared to argue. He cut her off. "Besides, I would not date Jessica if she was the last woman on earth."

Michelle's mouth worked in soundless frustration for a moment, then her eyes narrowed and she tossed her black locks. "You're really stupid," she said with finality.

"It's a handicap I've learned to live with," he shot back. The light of hope was completely gone from her face. She looked downright hostile.

"Men," she said, loading that tiny word with a mountain of disdain and frustration. She marched off with her nose in the air.

Jessica had defiantly donned her oldest T-shirt and her overall shorts. She bent over her bed and blotted lemonade off the sundress she had laid out in front of her. She knew, from her long experience with natural remedies and recipes, that lemon was nature's bleach. Nothing at all to worry about.

Where was a good worry when she needed it most? To take her mind off other things, like the moment of mad defiance that had made her decide no bloomers at all were better than one of the perfectly acceptable white, high-waisted, *comfortable* cotton panties that filled her bureau drawer.

And what had made her put on that silly sundress? She'd bought it on a whim, a year ago, thinking it made her look sexy, not thinking she had absolutely no reason—make that desire—to look sexy.

So, for a woman with no reason and no desire to look sexy, could that possibly have been *her* sashaying out across her garden, sans underwear, as if she were going to an upscale party in a place quite a bit less Victorian than, well, Victoria, B.C.?

Jessica knew the horrible truth! After being caught out in her sexless pajamas the first day Brian had arrived to work on the pond, she had been determined to show him every line and detail of the new and improved her. Except she'd ended up showing him even more than she planned. She was not sure what had happened to her resolve to quickly get rid of him. It had melted like butter left out in the sun.

Well, that was it. She was done playing games with him and with herself. The past was over, and she would only make a fool of herself by trying to change an impression that had been formed fourteen years ago. Besides, that impression said far more about him than her.

Superficial oaf. Too bad he looked so good without a shirt on that he could make a woman forget her senses—not to mention her drawers—entirely. That settled it, though. She had come face-to-face with her own weakness, and she wasn't giving in to it again. She was hiding out inside her cottage until he left for good. She would creep out in the night and water and harvest and weed. She didn't care if it was weeks away. She could not be around him. She simply lost her head and gave away her power too readily.

She had not grown and matured at all in the last fourteen years if she could still *yearn* for that man in ways that were totally unbecoming.

He'd asked her for a date because his niece thought it was a good idea? And the truth was that she had been sorely tempted to say yes. Did she not have an ounce of pride?

Yes, she did. An ounce of pride, and a hint of steel. Just enough to carry her through that horrible moment of terrifying temptation, just enough to form the words, Not if you were the last man on earth. As she blotted her dress, she remembered the one redeeming part of the whole episode: the shocked look in his eyes. She savored it.

He couldn't believe Jessica had turned him down.

"Jessica?"

She wanted to hide from the whole world, including his niece. Instead, she tried to paste on her blandest expression.

"In here."

Michelle came into her bedroom, inspected the dress, and then flopped on the bed. "Are you going to be able to fix it?"

Her life or the damned dress? "Lemon is nature's bleach," she said, addressing only the stain.

Michelle, who up until this point had been a sponge for information, looked not the least interested in nature's bleach.

"You know," Michelle said sadly, "I never thought I'd say this, but I feel really sorry for my uncle."

Don't bite, Jessica ordered herself, but she shot a look at the girl on her bed. Michelle looked genuinely distressed.

"What is it, Michelle?"

"Since my mom and dad died…" her voice cracked, and Jessica abandoned the dress to sit on the bed beside Michelle and stroke her hair "…he's different. When he used to come visit us, he was so much fun. He was always laughing and teasing. He always had really pretty girlfriends."

Just what I most wanted to know.

"But now, he always seems so somber. He never goes out anymore. He doesn't have a girlfriend. The last time he went out with someone her name was Bambi, and she's the one all the blond jokes were created for. But, that was four months ago, even though women phone for him lots."

Why did the fact that lots of women phoned for him make Jessica feel slightly sick to her stomach? Because she could easily be one of them? Throwing herself at him? Underwearless and shameless? A girl named Bambi might be able to get away with such a lack of restraint. The rest of the world, including Jessica, no.

"I think," Michelle continued gravely, "he's scared of being happy. I am, too."

It was a very deep observation for one so young, and Jessica could feel a lump of emotion building in her own throat.

"When I got the puppy, it was like something in me said, okay, I'm going to try this business of caring one more time. And then when O'Henry got sick…"

"Oh, baby," Jessica whispered.

"But look at O'Henry today. Did you see him chasing his tail this morning? Running after the seagulls? It was worth taking the chance."

"I'm glad you think so."

"You see, I think Unkie asking you out was the same thing as me saying okay to O'Henry. It's like he was saying he was going to give life another chance."

"It wasn't even his idea!" Jessica protested.

"Ha. You don't know him. He only does what he wants.

I've made lots of suggestions, let me tell you. I wanted to paint my bedroom this awesome shade of indigo. No way to that. And I wanted Chocolate Jamberries for breakfast cereal, and guess what I got? Raisin Bran. So, it's not as if he puts himself out for me. If he asked you out, it was because he wanted to, not because I suggested it."

"Well, just the same, Michelle, it's not a good idea. I'm not his type."

"I think he might need to rethink his type."

"That's not for you to decide."

"You wouldn't say that if you'd seen Bambi. Don't they put size restrictions on implants?"

"Michelle!"

"Jessica! It's not as if Uncle Brian asked you to marry him. He just asked you out. That's not such a big deal, is it?"

If she said it was, Michelle would go right back to her uncle and report that getting asked out was a big deal for Jessica. Which it might be, depending on how *big deal* was defined. She had not been on a date in three years. She supposed that made it a big deal.

But out loud she said, "Of course it's not a big deal."

"Uncle Brian is in such a sad, lonely place. I guess I thought if it wasn't such a big deal, you wouldn't mind helping him out."

"I don't think going on a date will fix anything that's bothering your uncle, Michelle." But Jessica registered the truth in what Michelle was saying. That was what was different about Brian. His eyes. They were no longer lit with mischief the way they had been when he was a boy. Gone was that devilish hint of laughter, that look that said he was the boy most likely to embrace an adventure. Now there was loneliness in them, distance, as if he held himself away from a world he had once danced with.

"Of course one date wouldn't help, 'cause it's not a big deal. But don't you think that him asking you to go out with him is a step in the right direction? Kind of like saying yes to life, the way I did with O'Henry?"

"I guess it might be," Jessica agreed, feeling the trap closing around her. She wanted to play a small part in putting the sparkle back in his eyes.

"You could go out there and tell him you've changed your mind," Michelle pleaded. "Please?"

It was craziness, and she knew it. And yet there was something shining in that girl's eyes that Jessica found irresistible. Hope.

She sighed. "Oh, okay," she said.

Michelle bounced up to her knees, threw her arms around Jessica and hugged her hard and long.

It almost made it worth it, though that's not how it felt when she strode across the yard in her most worn-out overall shorts, her wild hair flattened wetly against her head, not a drop of makeup on her face.

She stopped just short of where a pond might be someday. At the moment, it was a horrible mess of piled earth. Brian was way down deep in a hole.

"Is this going to be a pond or a swimming pool?" she asked dubiously, skirting around her mission. "That looks like the eight-foot end."

"It's a tunnel to China," he said darkly. "I'm escaping. From women. Story of my life."

So, her refusal had stung him. On a personal level or because it was Jessica who had said no to him?

"You should have started digging after Bambi. You could have been there by now."

A shovelful of dirt landed a little too close to her feet. "Her name wasn't Bambi. Jeez, Michelle has a big mouth."

He was still shirtless. Sweat gleamed on his hard muscles. There was a streak of dirt on his face, and another painted a broad band across his rippled belly. His jeans were muddy and clung to the hard line of his butt. He looked all man, strong and vigorous, not the least bit lonely or broken. The man least in need of help from anyone, let alone the homely girl from his past.

"I changed my mind," Jessica said in a rush.

The furious shoveling stopped. He went very still. He rested his hands on top of the shovel, and then his chin on his hands and gazed at her with unreadable dark eyes.

"I guess we could go on a date," she said stiffly.

For a moment she had the terrible feeling he was going to tell her he wouldn't go out with her now if she was the last woman on earth.

Of course, she wasn't clothed in lemonade-saturated transparent clothing, either.

"Okay," he said, after a long moment, and then turned his back to her and went back to work.

She glared at him darkly for a moment, then muttered, "Okay," and turned on her heel and left.

A week later she regretted the decision immensely. The date had been set. Now, dressed in brand-new underwear—bikini panties and a lace bra that appeared to be made of spider webs—she pulled yet another outfit over her head. She yanked open the bathroom door and went into her bedroom.

Michelle was on her tummy on Jessica's bed, flipping through the pages of *City Woman,* a magazine Jessica detested for its portrayal of women as too thin, too slick and too superficial. O'Henry was tucked under her arm, wriggled as close to Michelle as he could get.

The dog wasn't allowed on the bed, but that seemed to be the least of Jessica's problems.

The biggest was that Michelle had announced she was pretty sure Brian was taking Jessica to Smuggler's Lair, a very exclusive beachfront restaurant outside of Victoria.

"McDonald's would have been fine!" Jessica had moaned.

Now, Michelle was vetting her wardrobe. She glanced up at the latest offering and rolled her eyes.

"Jessica! A peach pantsuit? You know what that says?"

"Wal-Mart, $39.95?" Jessica guessed morosely.

"Nun on vacation!"

"Oh, I'm improving," Jessica said sarcastically. "I think nun-on-vacation is a distinct improvement over librarian-at-book-conference, and sixty-five-year-old-spinster-visiting-lonely-hearts-club-for-the-first-time, don't you?"

Michelle giggled, and somehow that simple girlish sound made this whole exercise somehow worthwhile.

"Can't we go shopping?" Michelle pleaded. "Please? It won't cost a lot. I promise. I'll help you."

Jessica should have had the good sense to remember how Michelle's help had got her into this mess in the first place. But again, she found the light in Michelle's eyes hard to resist. Such a simple, normal thing. A young girl wanting to go shopping.

From the look of Michelle's own wardrobe—blouses too short at the wrists and a smidgen too tight across the bust, pants too short at the ankles—the girl had not shown any interest in shopping for a long, long time.

"Okay," Jessica said, "but here's the deal. If I buy something, you buy something."

"Sure," Michelle said. "Uncle Brian gave me his credit card."

"Did you plan this all along?"

"Who, me?" she said innocently.

And then they both dissolved into helpless giggles.

Brian stared at the clothes laid out on his bed. A pair of dark trousers with a knifelike crease down the front, a black leather belt, a gray sport shirt with a discreet emblem over the chest. The emblem said expensive.

It also said these were not his clothes. He was going to have to lay down the law with Michelle. She was taking over his life. It was bad enough that she'd talked him into making reservations at the Smuggler's Lair when he would have been just as happy with McDonald's. Now, he was going to be the victim of a makeover?

"Michelle!" he yelled. "Can you explain this?"

She came and opened his bedroom door, slipped in. "The clothes? Oh, they're a present from me."

"A present from you," he repeated, but felt his desire to lay down the law evaporate. Something wonderful was happening to his niece, and it nearly blinded him now. This was the first time she'd been home in a week.

She was radiant. Her cheeks were full of healthy color. Her eyes glowed. Her makeup was light, and her hair was pulled back in a wholesome ponytail.

Maybe it was having the dog returned from the dead, or

maybe it was working in the sunshine and the garden every-day, or maybe it was the outfit she had on: it was pretty. Red shorts, a red-striped T-shirt, something a happy, well-adjusted thirteen-year-old would wear.

He knew the truth about the transformation. Most of it was her friendship with Jessica. From his outpost at the pond, he caught glimpses of them, heads together, bent over some plant, playing with the steadily strengthening pup. He heard the soft sounds of their voices and their sudden squeals of laughter.

He told himself, grouchily, in those moments, that he should be happy that his niece was being healed. But still, he felt excluded from the circle of their laughter. Jessica seemed determined to avoid him ever since she had said yes to the date—he supposed just in case he thought her saying yes had been personal.

"Is that new, too?" he asked of her outfit.

She laughed. "You don't notice things like that."

"Let me tell you, any change from black is worthy of notice."

"Do you like what I got for you?" she asked.

"I like blue jeans and sweatshirts. How did you get this? Somehow your allowance wouldn't do it."

"I borrowed some. From your credit card. Remember? You lent it to me to go shopping?"

"For you. I didn't authorize this."

"I'm going to pay for it. It's a present."

"How are you going to pay for it?" he asked. "There must be a hundred bucks worth of clothes here."

"Didn't I tell you? Jessica's showing me how to make bouquets of fresh-cut flowers. I took some to the Rain's Market on the corner, and they bought them all! I made fifteen dollars already!"

He had to duck his head to hide his feelings. His niece was making money—her very first little business—and she wanted to spend the profit on him?

"I can't wait to see the clothes on you," she said. "Are you excited?"

"Thrilled," he lied gruffly. "Get out of here."

He put on the clothes and eyed his reflection glumly. They were not his style at all. Good grief, he looked like a doctor going golfing. But he didn't have the heart to say that to his niece, who gave him last minute instructions all the way out the door.

"And don't forget to pull back her chair. And don't talk about your truck. Or how great the new cord for the pump is."

"Hey, I've done this once or twice before," he said. But he had to admit, he didn't feel like he had ever done it before.

He felt like an adolescent boy, awkward and shy and like he didn't have a clue what to do. He hated this. How on earth had this happened to him? By the time he got to Jessica's house he was nursing a fairly healthy resentment.

He wished he'd brought flowers, something to hold up in front of him, but of course flowers would have been utterly ridiculous given what she did for a living. A box of chocolates? Why hadn't Michelle thought of that? She'd thought of everything else.

With no flowers and no chocolates, he walked slowly to the door. He felt like a kid going to school for the first time—trapped, scared, bad-tempered.

He knocked on the door.

He heard a little flurry of activity and then silence. He

knocked again, and this time he caught the quick slide of the front drape as it cracked open and then closed.

"Jessica?"

He heard the tap of shoes across wooden floors. The door opened a crack. She crooked her head around the door.

"I can't do this," she whispered and then shut the door. He heard the tap of her heels retreating.

It was a dream come true! She didn't want to do it, either. He should run down the walk, clicking his heels.

Instead, he found his hand on the doorknob. He opened it, stuck his head in. "Jessica?" he called tentatively.

No answer.

He stepped inside. He had not used this entrance to her house before. Even in the gathering darkness, he sensed how cozy a space this was, how welcoming. Wooden floors, bookcases, handwoven rugs.

"Jessica?"

His eyes adjusted to the dark, and he now saw her sitting on the couch, her arms curled around her bare knees.

His jaw dropped. He was not sure he had ever seen anyone or anything quite so beautiful.

Jessica sat there, looking self-conscious and resentful in a dress concocted of turquoise film. The dress left one slender shoulder bare. It hugged her frame and hinted of her delectable curves as it swirled fully down to the perfect swell of her calves. A fine gold chain was at her throat and it made him notice the pulse that beat wildly there.

"You look beautiful," he said hoarsely, coming slowly toward her.

"That's good, because I feel like an idiot."

"You do?"

"Absolutely. I'm too old for this. I gave up on Cinderella dreams a long, long time ago."

"That's good, because just between you and I…" He flopped down on the couch beside her. "I'm no prince. Even if you kiss me."

Her eyes went very wide at that. Her gaze darted to his lips, moved away. "Well, don't worry about that," she said. "I'm not kissing you because I'm not even going out with you."

"Why not?"

"I was just trying to make Michelle happy," she confessed. "I've come to my senses. I can't use my life to make her happy. Not that it would work anyway."

"She talked me into it, too."

"Haven't we had this conversation before? It was insulting last time, too."

"Well, no more insulting for you than for me," he said. "No man wants to hear that a beautiful woman agreed to go out with him to make his niece happy."

"Except I'm not really beautiful," she said and yanked at the turquoise. "This is not me."

"No," he said softly. "But this is." He touched the corners of her eyes, the fullness of her lip. Her lip actually trembled under his fingertip.

Reminding him he had a gift for wrecking things fragile.

He yanked his hand away.

"Don't worry," she said, "I'm no princess. And just between you and me…the glass slippers hurt like hell."

He looked down at her feet. They were tiny, and the shoes were high-heeled and flimsy and elevated her to a goddess. There was something about her feet, whether encased in glass slippers or digging bare into the dirt that made his mouth go dry.

"You know, I haven't done much of this kind of thing. How about if I go change into some jeans and sneakers and we go to McDonald's?" she said wistfully.

"Ha. Are you going to be the one to break it to Michelle?"

"No thanks. I'm not that courageous."

"Me, either."

But suddenly he wanted very much to take her to Smuggler's Lair, and not for Michelle, either. The words, that she had given up her Cinderella dreams, stuck with him. He had been part of that caste system that had excluded her, hurt her. Perhaps part of the reason fate had delivered him and a dog and a troubled teen to her doorstep was that he owed amends.

He was being given a second chance to do the right thing. It was the rarest of opportunities, and if anyone should be able to have Cinderella dreams, it should be her. It was a simple thing. Give her a night out, make up somehow for all the one's she had missed, the prom night and the grad night and the Christmas Ball.

They'd been horrible events, stuffy and awkward, each and every one. He'd usually ended up drunk on the gym floor with his date, some girl in taffeta with a flower pinned to her bosom who glared at him in a way that was all too familiar.

But Jessica didn't have to know that.

He crooked his elbow at her. "My lady, let me escort you to the carriage."

She hesitated, shook her head ruefully, and then put her arm through his. She wobbled a little on the shoes, as they crossed her living room. She leaned into him, and his breath caught at the soft nakedness of her shoulder touching his arm. But then she seemed to find herself, and by the time they got to the truck, she'd regained her confidence.

She grinned at his truck. "It looks more like a pumpkin than a carriage."

"That's okay. I'm more like a frog than a prince," he said and opened the door for her.

She looked at him for a long moment before she got in the truck. She touched his cheek softly with her fingertips and said, "No, you aren't, Brian."

Somehow those simple words and the sincerity with which they were spoken changed everything. In the blink of an eye, he went from wanting to give her a wonderful night out to wanting only to save himself.

They arrived at Smuggler's Lair, and he could tell she loved it—set as it was amongst rocks and plants, perched above the ocean. The interior decor was subtle and rich, and they were led to an exquisite table overlooking the ocean. Brian couldn't help but notice that Jessica turned more than her fair share of heads, a fact to which she seemed charmingly oblivious.

They settled at the table, studied the menus, ordered wine.

When their menus had been removed she looked ruefully at him. "Now what?" she asked.

"Well, we, uh, talk to each other."

"About?"

He wanted to say, *about you*. He wanted to say, *tell me everything about you*.

He'd said that a million times to women, but not once had he cared, really. He was astonished to find out he really wanted to know. Every single thing about her. He wanted to know how she'd survived those years of high school, what events had shaped her and made her so strong and such a survivor. He wanted to know which of those flowers she grew was her favorite and what she dreamed of before she drifted into sleep at night.

And the fact that he wanted to know those things scared the living daylights out of him. That and the fact that he was remembering the soft puffiness of her lip beneath his finger, and wondering as he sat across from her what those lips would feel like beneath his.

But some things he already knew about her. He knew, from the cottage, that she didn't commit lightly. She cared deeply for the things she took the time to plant. He had seen that in her relationship with his niece, in the way her hands touched O'Henry.

She was not a woman you could ask, tell me about you, unless it meant something. Unless you planned for it to go somewhere.

And he just wasn't that kind of guy.

Save yourself, he repeated inwardly. And he knew just how to do it, too.

He lifted his wine glass to her. "Let's talk about me," he suggested, paraphrasing the title of a song he found particularly entertaining.

She obviously did not tune into the country station, because she didn't see the humor. She leaned forward, listening.

Intently. As if she thought he had something to say. Something important. Or deep.

Of course, he had neither.

So, he told her stupid stories about work that made him come off as insensitive and far more macho than he was. Bambi or Tiffany, or whatever her name was, had leaned forward nicely, revealing even more of her décolleté, as he'd plunged into these very same stories. Her long red talons had bitten into his upper arm. Her eyes had been wide and star-filled.

But Jessica wasn't leaning forward. She was clutching her wineglass a little too tightly and he could see her probing him with her eyes. He knew the truth: if anyone could get to who he really was, it would be her.

But was he ready to go there?

He was disappointing her. He knew it. That was the game plan. Disappoint now instead of disappoint later. He tried to feel thrilled that it was so obviously working, but in his soul he had to fight down the regret.

And then, when he was pretty sure he couldn't have a more disastrous evening, he was proven wrong.

Because over her shoulder, at the table right behind them, he saw an elderly man clutch suddenly at his chest and fall out of his chair.

He got up so hastily, he knocked over the wine. From his peripheral vision he saw the wine running out onto her dress and the astounded look on her face as he raced by her.

My personal gift, he told himself, as he arrived at the prone body of the man collapsed on the floor. *Disaster. And I deliver.*

Chapter Six

For a moment, back there at her cottage, when Brian had touched her eyelids and her lips with the newly formed calluses on his fingertips and looked at her so deeply, Jessica had felt helpless against his power. She had felt the leashed strength in his touch and had nearly melted under that combination of power and tenderness.

Momentarily, insanely, she had been swept up in a deep desire to believe in the possibility of happily-ever-after in real life.

He was setting her straight now, though, by going from prince to frog in the blink of an eye. Why was she disappointed? He had even warned her. She should have felt nothing but relief!

She had thought that the man who teased the back of her mind for fourteen years had been confirmed by that brief touch, in that lingering look. But it was, after all, just a fantasy. A fantasy she had fueled by watching him run around

An Important Message
from the Editors

Dear Reader,

Because you've chosen to read one of our fine romance novels, we'd like to say "thank you!" And, as a special way to thank you, we've selected two more of the books you love so well, plus an exciting Mystery Gift, to send you absolutely FREE!

Please enjoy them with our compliments...

Pam Powers

Peel off Seal and Place Inside...

How to validate your Editor's
FREE GIFT
"Thank You"

1. Peel off gift seal from front cover. Place it in space provided at right. This automatically entitles you to receive 2 FREE BOOKS and a fabulous mystery gift.

2. Send back this card and you'll get 2 brand-new Silhouette Romance® novels. These books have a combined cover price of $7.98 or more in the U.S. and $9.00 in Canada, but they are yours to keep absolutely free.

3. There's no catch. You're under no obligation to buy anything. We charge nothing—ZERO—for your first shipment. And you don't have to make any minimum number of purchases—not even one!

4. The fact is, thousands of readers enjoy receiving their books by mail from the Silhouette Reader Service™. They enjoy the convenience of home delivery...they like getting the best new novels at discount prices BEFORE they're available in stores...and they love their *Heart to Heart* subscriber newsletter featuring author news, horoscopes, recipes, book reviews and much more!

5. We hope that after receiving your free books you'll want to remain a subscriber. But the choice is yours— to continue or cancel, any time at all! So why not take us up on our invitation, with no risk of any kind. You'll be glad you did!

6. Remember...just for validating your Editor's Free Gift Offer, we'll send you THREE gifts, *ABSOLUTELY FREE!*

GET A Free MYSTERY GIFT...

*SURPRISE MYSTERY GIFT COULD BE YOURS **FREE** AS A SPECIAL "THANK YOU" FROM THE EDITORS OF SILHOUETTE*

Visit us online at
www.eHarlequin.com

The Editor's "Thank You" Free Gifts Include:

- Two BRAND-NEW romance novels!
- An exciting mystery gift!

PLACE FREE GIFT SEAL HERE

Yes I have placed my Editor's "Thank You" seal in the space provided above. Please send me 2 free books and a fabulous Mystery Gift. I understand I am under no obligation to purchase any books, as explained on the back and on the opposite page.

309 SDL DZ6N   **209 SDL DZ63**

FIRST NAME

LAST NAME

ADDRESS

APT.#

CITY

STATE/PROV.

ZIP/POSTAL CODE

(S-R-07/04)

Thank You!

◀ **DETACH AND MAIL CARD TODAY!** ▼

The Silhouette Reader Service™ — Here's how it works:

Accepting your 2 free books and gift places you under no obligation to buy anything. You may keep the books and gift and return the shipping statement marked "cancel." If you do not cancel, about a month later we'll send you 6 additional books and bill you just $22.84 per shipment in the U.S., or $26.18 per shipment in Canada, plus applicable taxes if any.* That's a savings of over 10% off the price of all 6 books! You may cancel at any time, but if you choose to continue, every month we'll send you 6 more books, which you may either purchase at the discount price or return to us and cancel your subscription.

*Terms and prices subject to change without notice. Sales tax applicable in N.Y. Canadian residents will be charged applicable provincial taxes and GST.

If offer card is missing write to: The Silhouette Reader Service, 3010 Walden Ave., P.O. Box 1867, Buffalo, NY 14240-1867

BUSINESS REPLY MAIL
FIRST-CLASS MAIL   PERMIT NO. 717-003   BUFFALO, NY

POSTAGE WILL BE PAID BY ADDRESSEE

SILHOUETTE READER SERVICE
3010 WALDEN AVE
PO BOX 1867
BUFFALO NY 14240-9952

NO POSTAGE
NECESSARY
IF MAILED
IN THE
UNITED STATES

in her yard half-naked for the past few weeks. If she wanted to fantasize about half-naked men, to create fictions that matched their eyes and their chests, then she would really be much wiser to buy one of those calendars.

Here was the reality: He apparently thought being in a shoot-out—where lives, including his own, were at risk—was fun. He thought arresting a pathetic old woman for shoplifting was entertaining. He thought tales of his speed and agility would impress her, as if he was still captain of the high school football team.

Under all that bluff and bravado, she thought she saw something else. But hadn't that always been her problem when it came to him? She thought she could see strength, integrity, spirit. But if those qualities existed in him, he seemed determined not to show them now.

She wasn't sixteen anymore. Back then it had seemed rather romantic to read characteristics into Brian that his actions did not confirm. Now at the ripe age of thirty-one it would be naive to insist on seeing things that were not there. The ancient shoplifter had probably thought he had nice eyes, too! She might have seen the kindness lurking in their depths, or the loneliness. That poor old soul might have felt a moment's liking for Officer Brian Kemp, right before he snapped on the cuffs and said, "Ma'am, you are under arrest."

No wonder the old gal had hit him with a frozen fish. Undoubtedly he had deserved it. She looked at him narrowly. If she had a frozen fish, she might hit him with it, too! Chateaubriand didn't seem like it would make quite the same statement, so she took a dainty bite and tried not to roll her eyes as he told her about some child on a bicycle with a stolen stereo under his arm.

How could he tell these horrible stories without being embarrassed? A kid on a bike was not public enemy number one! In fact, her sympathies seemed to be leaning toward the criminals.

"And then the kid rode the bike over a cliff!" Brian exclaimed. "I couldn't believe it. I went and looked over and it must have been a twenty-foot drop, and there he was, after landing upright, peddling away. Well, I thought, if he can do it so can I. So I jumped…"

He stopped abruptly, midsentence, then catapulted from his chair.

In the absence of a frozen fish, Jessica had the very bad grace to hope a bee had stung him. Unfortunately, his knee knocked the table, and the wine went over with a crash. It was a perfect conclusion to a disastrous evening, Jessica thought, looking down at the wine splashing down the front of her dress. She grabbed the bottle and set it upright but obviously the damage was done.

Red. Possibly, if she ordered some club soda immediately, she might be able to get it out. But maybe it would be better to leave it in. The stain would serve as a reminder that fairy tales were just that. Stories. Lovely dreamy fantasies, with absolutely no grounds in reality. Prince Charming inevitably had an ego, or spilled wine or lemonade on your dress, or…

"Call 9-1-1. Do it now."

Brian's voice was calm, hard, full of authority. Jessica whirled in her chair.

The waiter was flapping a white serviette, chattering hysterically, and punching numbers into his cell phone. An elderly woman seated at the table behind Jessica began to cry. Staff were coming from all corners of the restaurant. And in the center of everything, Brian was on the floor with a gray-haired gentleman who was very, very still.

Her eyes fastened on Brian, a pillar of calm in a sea of chaos. Jessica rose so abruptly that the newly righted wine fell back over and spilled the rest of its contents on the floor.

She barely noticed that. She couldn't believe that she had been so lost in her own world that she had missed the drama behind her. Though, really, it had only been seconds since Brian left the table.

She pushed quickly through the throng forming around the scene and went to her knees near the elderly man's head.

She glanced at Brian. His features were cast in the iron of concentration, reflecting a breathtaking singleness of focus. He knelt at the man's side, then brought his interlaced fingers down on the man's chest and pumped, hard. Counted, then pumped again.

Jessica took a long, steadying breath, then looked once more at Brian. She allowed some of his strength to bolster her own. Firmly she placed one hand on the fallen man's shoulder and another on his brow. She cleared everything from her mind, even the sight of Brian. Though something about his intensity as he crouched over that man weighed on her mind, tried to tell her what she most needed to know…

Still, as she closed her eyes she felt the beginning of the light, bright and pure around her. Her fingertips began to tingle, and she could feel warmth emanating from her palms. Behind her closed eyes she saw the prisms of extraordinary color. The energy vibrated out through her fingers, tingling, warm, alive. She could feel the energy moving around the man on the floor. Cold and darkness repelled what she was offering. She focused on the light, trusted it and gave herself to it.

She had no idea how much time had passed. She was only peripherally aware of Brian, his voice giving quiet commands, yet she could feel how powerfully their energy was joined. The rest—the crowd around them, the far off scream of a siren—she blocked almost entirely from her awareness.

She knew the exact moment the light pierced the lifeless body in front of her. An amazing feeling washed over her, a kind of awe for the world and how it worked and for powers seen and unseen. She let the feeling of extraordinary peace embrace her. She kept her eyes closed and her hands quiet on the man.

"I've got a heartbeat," Brian said. He moved beside her, and she opened her eyes when his shoulder touched hers. She watched as he unhesitatingly tilted back the man's head, covered his lips with his own and breathed his life force into the man.

Moments later, paramedics raced into the room, and she was flung aside and forgotten in the melee of activity. Brian briefed them. Then he reached down for her hand, helping her to her feet.

He stared at her intently, and she gazed back at him just as intently.

The truth: when he was bent over that man, she had seen exactly what she needed to see in Brian. And it was not that he was the man who tried to entertain her with macho stories from work. It was that he was exactly the man she had always seen promised in the mysterious depth of his eyes.

It was this man, who stood before her, calm and strong. One who had chosen his work, not because it was exciting, as he had led her to believe, or because he was power hungry, controlling, or an adrenaline junkie. Brian was a policeman because it allowed him to serve using his unique gift.

And his gift was courage. It was the ability to bring order to chaos. It was the ability to remain calm and think quickly and clearly in a crisis. This is what she had glimpsed all those years ago, when they had stood shoulder to shoulder working on that dog. The authentic Brian. Not that suave boy who made quick jokes, kissed girls in the corridor sheltered by the Coke machine, or drove his pickup way too fast.

And not the man who had sat across the table from her, spinning tales intended to entertain while keeping his most private self locked away.

The real Brian stood before her, a man stripped of his defenses, a man of soul so deep it could be frightening. Captivating. Addicting.

"Are you okay?" he asked quietly, and he touched her bare shoulder. "You're trembling."

She nodded, brushing away the tears that were forming in her eyes. "I'm fine." His hand felt like fire where it rested on her shoulder, the kind of fire that beckoned after a storm, promising warmth and safety and comfort.

"Sir, thank you so much." It was the maitre d'. "Of course, your meal is on the house tonight. Can I bring you another bottle of wine? You saved that man's life! What's your name? I'm going to tell the newspapers."

The man's voice was an intrusion on the world they had entered into. This private place, almost sacred, was where they were both stripped of their defenses and where they could see, finally, each other and the truth.

Jessica could feel Brian's gaze, intense, on her face.

He turned and spoke softly to the maitre d', and slipped his arm protectively around her shoulder. Then he said, "Come on. Let's get a breath of fresh air."

Moments later he took her out a side door of the restaurant and was leading her down a stone staircase outside. His hand remained in hers longer than was necessary, and again she felt the seductive pull of his callused fingertips and palms.

The staircase led to a beautiful crescent of beach. The tips of the waves were washed in moonlight as they dissolved on the silvered sand. The air smelled fresh and held the tang of the sea.

Brian pressed her lightly on her shoulder, and she sank down onto the sand. He sat behind her, his legs forming a V around her. He pulled her back into the comforting wall of his chest and laced his hands on her lap. "I'll keep you warm," he said.

Fulfilling the promise of his touch: warmth, safety, comfort.

"The sand will wreck the dress, but I'm placing bets it's ruined anyway, right?" he asked. But she knew he was only seeking diversion from the intensity of that experience, trying to bring them back to a world where stains on dresses mattered. She was not ready to go back there yet.

"Tell me how you really felt about that eighty-three-year-old woman shoplifter," she said softly.

"Nah, let's talk about your dress."

"No."

He was silent, and she thought perhaps he would refuse the level of intimacy she was inviting him to share. But she didn't rush him, instead she looked at the moon and luxuriated in the feel of his arms around her. The hard wall of his chest at her back and the strength of his legs enclosed her. Then, she allowed herself to feel again that tingle of healing energy.

"Sad," he finally said, the word drawn out of him reluctantly. She sighed, satisfied. "And at the bank robbery?"

"Scared. And as I chased down the boy with the bike? Old and worn out."

She nodded, knowing truth when she heard it.

After a long time, he went on, his voice soft in the night. "Jessica, I can't save them. I can't fix anybody or anything. If I thought about it too much I couldn't even survive. Sensitivity would be a flaw in my business, probably a fatal one."

The confession did not make her think of weakness, but rather, of strength. It was an act of trust, and she felt he did not give that often and certainly not lightly. He was finally showing her a glimpse of the real Brian. And it was everything she had known it would be.

"You saved one tonight," she reminded him softly. "You fixed someone tonight."

He sighed and his arms tightened around her. "He probably won't survive the night, Jessica. Odds are against it."

"I think he will."

"Crystal ball or just a guess?"

"Maybe a bit of both."

"Think that then, but don't call the hospital to find out. That's how you survive. You detach. You do the best you can, and then you let go."

"I'm not sure I could ever be like that."

"Good. I like that about you. But don't apply for the police department."

She chuckled softly. "It wasn't on my list of things to do this week."

"You know most of the girls love my cop stories," he said gruffly.

"Bambi was impressed?"

"Am I ever going to live her down?"

"Not likely. Brian, I'm not most girls."

"I know, Jessica. I should have known better. You never were."

"I would have been if I could have been," she admitted.

"I'm glad you couldn't make yourself into something you weren't. Very glad. You might have lost everything that was best about you, including whatever it was that saved that man. I know I did the CPR but I had this feeling that I didn't really save him. You did."

"No," she said firmly, "You did, Brian."

"Then why is it that, a split second before he started breathing, I looked at your face and there was this light shining in it? You were almost smiling. As if you already knew."

She shrugged. She did not feel quite ready to leave the intensity of the experience, but she did not want to dissect it, either.

"Jessica, you did it, didn't you? You healed something in that man, the very same way you did with the dog, all those years ago."

Suddenly, that other scene was vivid in her mind. The screech of the truck tires as she got off the bus beside her driveway, the yelp of the dog, the handsome boy she had seen so many times at school as he got out of his truck—distraught at what he had done. He didn't really even see her. Just the dog.

"I killed him," he said flatly.

"I don't think so." She had knelt over the dog, felt the life force strong within it, picked it up gently. "Can you come with me to my house?"

There had been an old garden shed with a table in it, and they had taken the dog there. She had become aware as she worked over the dog, that Brian was seeing her. Brian Kemp, school heartthrob, was *seeing* her. And not as a social outcast. He was seeing her soul. And she could tell, in those enchanted moments, how much he had liked what he had seen.

After, they had sat out on the stoop watching the stars come up, talking effortlessly, laughing.

"I'll call," he had said. He had touched her chin with his fingertip and made her look deep into his eyes.

And those words had seemed like a vow. No, more. Like a ticket out of the miserable experience of her life. Her parents were dead. She was being raised by an eccentric maiden aunt. She was overweight; she was different; she was poor; she was teased. And that strange chance encounter had made her believe that she, Jessica Moran, the one the kids called witch and weirdo, could be loved. The interest that had flickered in his eyes had been like being thrown a life preserver when she had been drowning in the pool of her own loneliness.

She had waited. Even when he blew her off at school, she had hoped. She had hoped right until the day she saw him with Lucinda Potter backed into the corner by the Coke machine.

Lucinda was everything Jessica was not. Tall, slender, outrageously beautiful, outgoing.

And Brian Kemp had been kissing her with a passion completely out of place for a high school hallway. It hadn't seemed to matter to him one little bit that Lucinda was clearly unworthy of him—mean-spirited and superficial.

The bitterness of that memory was as strong as a bad taste in her mouth.

"I'm sorry," he said softly. "Of all the things I regret in my life, hurting you is just about at the top of my list."

She said nothing, afraid to accept his apology. If she let go of her residue of anger then what defense would she have left? In a way, she had been safer when he was spinning his tales at the table. In a way, she realized, she had been looking—and hard—for excuses not to like him, not to be swept away.

And here she was, despite her best efforts, swept away after all.

"I felt then exactly what I feel now," Brian continued softly, his voice low and sensual, close to her ear, stirring the hair on the nape of her neck. "I felt you were special. Deep. Real. More real than anything I had ever encountered before."

She was silent.

"Look, Jessica, I've been trying not to reopen old wounds, but could we put high school behind us? And what happened there? I was young. I didn't have a clue what to do with someone like you, something like that. I had no idea how rare it was, what a gift. When I was with you that night, I felt things I had never, ever felt before. Alive. Connected to the world in ways I didn't know human beings connected to the world. I said I would call, and I didn't and that had everything to do with me and nothing to do with you."

"I know that."

He took a deep breath. "This is what I want you to understand—you were lucky I never called. I wouldn't have been anything but a world of hurt to someone as tender as you. You're still tender, soft."

His hand, almost unconsciously, found the silk of soft skin on her naked shoulder and caressed it. He underscored the word *soft* with his fingertips.

"I'm tougher than you think," she protested, though his hand on her shoulder was making her feel weak.

"Maybe you are," he said, "but even then I knew you would require more of me than had ever been asked before. You would ask me to be better than I was. I would have to learn to see in a different way. A deeper way. I would have to give up believing all the things I believed to that point. I wasn't ready, Jessica."

She held her breath.

"And I'm not sure I'm ready now."

Before, she had been a young girl, frightened by the power of what had happened between them. She had been unsure that she was good enough, pretty enough, smart enough, cool enough to be with Brian Kemp.

Before, she had let him call all the shots. She had tossed in the towel without really entering the game.

She had felt she could not compete against opponents like Lucinda Potter.

She did not know if that had been a mistake, but she did know that she was not letting it unfold the same way this time. She was no longer the girl who stood on the sidelines waiting for life to notice her.

She had seen Brian Kemp. As he bent over that dying man, she had seen, unquestionably, who he really was. She knew he kept it hidden deep inside, this most vulnerable part of himself.

But she had seen it twice now. Once many years ago with the dog. And again tonight. And this time she was choosing not to walk away from the power of it. She did not want to.

She twisted in his arms, tilted her head toward him, and touched her lips to his. He tasted of wine and salt, wind and sand.

His lips tasted of a world she had not known, a world of sensuality and passion and promise.

His lips tasted of heaven.

At first he seemed startled. He answered tentatively, with exquisite tenderness.

But the texture of the kiss changed swiftly. Jessica could feel the tattoo of his heart increase in tempo. His hands became hard and urgent where they gripped her shoulders. His lips became more aggressive, demanding a response from her.

And she gave it readily, eagerly, answering the heat in him with her own fire. Then his tongue parted her lips and darted into the hollow of her mouth, and his hands slipped from her shoulders and stroked the cage of her ribs, the flatness of her belly.

Jessica had never felt so exquisitely tortured. Her need to know him as a man was naked and urgent within her. She allowed her own hands to explore the hard line of his thighs, the uncompromising line of his chest, the ripple of muscle in his arms, the line of his stomach.

His palm scraped the filmy fabric over her breast, and she went very still, frozen in exquisite sensation and desperate yearning. She broke the seal of his lips, tilted her head back and looked at him.

His eyes were dark with desire, she could feel the intensity of the heat rolling off his body.

"I want you," she said, startled by her own boldness and then delighted by it. She was no longer the girl who had waited passively for the phone call that never came. She tried out the new her by pressing her fingertips to the hem of his shirt, tugging it from where it was tucked into his trousers, slipping her hands underneath. Touching the taut silkiness of his skin was nearly as erotic as touching his lips.

"Take it off," she whispered, playing with her power, smiling when he slipped the shirt over his head. She ran her lips possessively over the hard nub of his nipple and the mound of a perfectly shaped pectoral muscle.

She felt him quiver beneath her and delighted again in her newfound power. She nipped him lightly. He groaned.

"I don't want to make love to you on the beach," he whispered hoarsely in her ear.

Make love to her? Of course that's what the statement *I want you* meant, even if she had meant it in a far deeper way. Still, of course that was where this was going. Why did she suddenly feel stunned, as if she had been swept away against her will?

The thoughts fled as his lips captured hers once more. He lifted her to her feet and brushed the sand from her dress. His hands lingered on her curves until she was trembling. He buried his face in her neck and set her away from him only for a moment while he pulled his shirt back over his head. Then he scooped her into his arms as though she weighed no more than a sprite. He carried her up the stone staircase, and, at the top of it, he covered her face with tiny tender kisses. He set her on her feet, and they skirted the restaurant on their way back to his truck.

He opened the door for her, but before she could get in, his lips found hers again. In the darkness, he pressed her against the seat of the truck, his lips owning her, branding her. He bent her back, his thigh pressing her intimately.

They broke apart only when a light from the restaurant door splashed across the parking lot. She saw his face, the heat and the hunger in it. She scrambled into the truck and waited for him to come around.

But he shut her door and stood for a long moment in the parking lot, looking at the stars. When he got in the truck, he looked at her, touched the wildness of her hair, and smiled with regret.

She felt the balance of power shifting, moving out of her court and into his. The question was, could she trust him with the control? Or would he leave her high and dry just like last time? The rational part of her knew this was a good time to find out—before anything irrevocable happened.

But the irrational part of her looked at his lips. She slid across the truck to him, tickled his ear with her tongue.

He put her gently away from him. "This isn't how we're going to play this one, Jessica."

"What?" she said, her breath still ragged. "What do you mean?"

"Jessica, I can kiss any woman in the world. It's generally what I do with women."

That black picture of him with Lucinda at the Coke machine inserted itself into her mind.

"I don't understand you," she said coolly.

"Help me be a better man, Jessica."

"How?"

"Let's back up a few steps. Let's get to know each other."

If he said *Let's just be friends* his buddies were going to be investigating a homicide in the parking lot of Smuggler's Lair in the morning.

But he didn't say that. He said, "If this whole thing hadn't been orchestrated by Michelle, what would you have wanted to do? What would you have chosen for a date? I have a feeling it's not chateaubriand at Smuggler's Lair."

So, she hadn't pulled it off. She looked ridiculous in the dress. She was a clumsy lover. He knew it wasn't her. He could see right through her.

Still, he didn't appear to be running away, either.

"So," he pressed. "If we were going to start all over again, what would you want to do? On a date?"

She hesitated, closed her eyes and tried to block out the memory of his lips. She couldn't. The taste of them was still on hers. With incredible discipline she turned her mind away from the passion of that kiss.

"First of all, I'd want it to be not like a date at all. No feeling awkward about the forks, no dressing up in finery fit for a princess." She slipped her feet out of the shoes and tucked them behind his seat.

He grinned. "I like you so far, except does no glass slipper mean no stolen kiss?"

"You already stole your kiss!" Frankly, he made a lousy kiss bandit because he could have stolen quite a few more before she would have objected.

"Don't distract me," he said sternly. "I got ahead of myself on the kiss thing, but I'm trying to make it up to you right now. So, what would you do? If we were starting all over?"

"I guess," she said slowly, thinking carefully, "what I'd really like to do is work side by side with you on that pond. Help pick the rocks and place them. And when we got hot and sweaty enough we could take inner tubes to a little creek behind my place and float in the sun."

The most attractive man on the island had asked her what she wanted to do on a dream date, and she had said she wanted to get all hot and sweaty?

Had she really changed at all from that awkward, hopeless teenager she had been? Physically, maybe. But inside?

"Would that be with or without bathing suits?" he asked wickedly.

"With!" she said so promptly and with such indignation they both laughed.

"You got a date, Jessica." He actually whistled as he drove her home, apparently that kiss not eating him alive from the inside the same way it was doing to her.

Somehow they were already at her place. He got out of the truck, came around and let her out. He walked her to the door, and kissed her very gently on the mouth.

When she reached hungrily for more, he put her aside.

"Uh-uh. For once in my life, I'm going to do something right."

She watched him as he got back in his truck. She was shivering, and it was not from the cool of the evening, either.

"How was it, Unkie?" Michelle asked eagerly.

"It was okay," he said.

"I want to know all about it! What did you eat?"

"Michelle, I am not going to be grilled about my love life by a thirteen-year-old. It's none of your business."

"Your *love life*?" Michelle breathed.

"I didn't mean it like that."

"Like what?" she asked innocently.

"Like I'm in love. I'm not. I never have been. I never will be."

"You haven't?" she asked, astounded.

"No," he said tersely.

Michelle looked at him, then shook her head. "That's very sad," she decided.

He decided it was a bad night indeed when two women got to that vulnerable place inside him that held sadness rather than glory.

"Could you at least tell me if you had fun?"

Fun. He thought of Jessica's lips and her eyes and the way she required more of him and the way she didn't fall for his stupid stories.

"A man had a heart attack, and I spilled wine all over Jessica trying to get to him." Much easier to recite a few facts than to explore the confusion inside of him.

And then she came and knelt beside me, and I looked at her face and I saw a light in it that made me feel as if my whole life had been empty and bereft.

"Was it a complete disaster?" Michelle asked, not the least surprised.

"The man lived."

"That's not what I meant!"

"Okay, it wasn't a complete disaster."

Michelle looked slightly relieved.

For some reason he told her, "We're going to try it again. But on our terms, this time. We're going to wear what we want and do what we want. That means no Michelle. No planning. No manipulating. No matchmaking."

"As if I would," she said, trying to act insulted, but her eyes were shining.

He hated that. He hated people relying on him to make them happy. He was an utter failure at it.

No doubt this whole thing was a mistake. A terrible mistake that was going to end badly with him hurting Jessica and Michelle.

"Oh, Aunt Lucy called tonight."

Brian felt every single cell in his body go on red alert. "What did she want?"

"She's flying in from T.O for a visit." Michelle rolled her

eyes. "She wants to help me shop for my back-to-school wardrobe. She said she's just like a fairy godmother."

Lucinda *was* his niece's godmother, but a less likely fairy godmother he could not envision. Weren't they generally short and plump with gray hair and half glasses?

When he'd seen Lucinda, his sister-in-law's best friend, at the funeral, she had been more striking even than in high school, and she had been plenty damned striking then.

After the service, Brian and Lucy had turned to each other, looking for something to fill the terrible emptiness. They had exchanged a few very passionate kisses. It had gone no further than those kisses because it had been a temporary release from a permanent pain, and they both had known it.

Hadn't they?

Her timing couldn't be worse. Two women with unfinished business in his life at the very same time? How had he offended the powers that be so much that he deserved this?

Chapter Seven

It was several days before Brian had a day off so that he could go out to Jessica's for their second date.

Meanwhile, he felt almost embarrassed by his preoccupation with her. Songs on the radio made him think of her. The sunset reminded him of her hair. He lay, restless, in his bed thinking about her lips and her hips and everything in between.

The first time he phoned her he felt a knot in his stomach the size of one of those boulders he was collecting for the edge of her pond.

"Uh," he said, feeling more awkward than he had since he was thirteen. "I just called to say hi."

He was calling a woman to say hi. He had the awful feeling that it led to other things, like football games interrupted and discussions of truck trade-ins.

But when she said "hi" back and he heard the happiness in her voice that he had called, the lump in his stomach dissolved and moved up to his throat. Making football into some kind of a religion suddenly seemed to be the dumb and desperate kind of thing a very lonely man did.

But aside from the fact that he felt like he might be willing to put football aside for Jessica, a more serious doubt had to be dealt with. Brian knew darn well he couldn't be trusted with anything as fragile as a woman's happiness, but he was barging ahead, anyway.

"I found some water lilies for the pond, today," Jessica told him. She described them in detail, and he shouldn't have found it the least bit interesting, but he did, interesting and endearing. Some women would have reserved her kind of enthusiasm for diamonds, or dream homes, or tickets to Céline Dion, but his sweet Jessica liked water lilies.

His. He contemplated that, stunned.

"What did you do today?" she asked.

"You know, the usual. Arrested an old lady, ran down a kid barely out of diapers."

She laughed. But then she said, "No, really."

And he told her how it had really been. Basically boring, except for that one moment after a car accident when he'd helped someone who was disoriented and afraid. And as he told Jessica about it, it felt as if everything was going to be okay, as if all was right in his world. The conversation flowed between them as naturally as if they'd been talking every day for the past fourteen years.

He did not know how she could make him laugh over a spider on her pillowcase or cookies burning in the oven, but she could. Laugh, and long to be with her.

"So what do you really think about my truck?" he asked suddenly.

"Your truck?" She laughed at the unexpected change of subject. "I love your truck."

"You're kidding, right?"

"No, I'm not."

"Sure. Tell me what you like about it." He was testing her. She could be pretending to like his truck. Women did things like that. Pretended to like everything you liked until they had you exactly where they wanted you and then *wham*.

"Okay, I like it that it's different from anything else you see on the road. Not out of a cookie cutter. I can't see you driving a cookie cutter kind of vehicle."

Damned right. "Anything else?"

"I like how it's old, but it's been treated so kindly that it still seems solid and safe and reliable. It's very comfortable. And I like the way it smells." She hesitated, and then said shyly, "I like the way your arm looks when you change gears."

He gulped. Before she threw him way off track, he asked the most important thing. "But if I told you I was trading it in on a Lamborghini, then what would you say?"

"Nothing. Because I'd never speak to you again."

It was at that precise moment that he knew exactly what was happening. He was falling in love with Jessica Moran.

And that amazing thought wiped Lucinda's impending arrival right out of his mind, not that a natural moment to insert it into the conversation had ever appeared, anyway.

After he hung up, he thought about it. Things were going so well. With his history for doing exactly the wrong thing, maybe Lucinda wasn't even something he *had* to tell Jessica. If he looked at the facts, that seemed rational. Michelle's godmother was coming. She was coming to see Michelle. She was staying in a hotel. There was a good chance, with careful planning, that Brian wouldn't even see her.

So why did Jessica have to know? Lucinda was part of a world Jessica had left behind, outstripped beautifully. Would it be a good idea to shove her painful past in her face if it was unnecessary?

Still, when he got out of his truck that bright Tuesday morning, and saw Jessica coming toward him, he didn't think it was good that the first thing he felt was a tiny little whisper of guilt about how he had never gotten around to telling her about Lucinda, who had arrived the night before.

But it was hard to hold a bad thought and look at Jessica at the same time. She was dressed for work in khaki shorts that showed off the shapely curves of her tanned legs. Her curls were partially hidden under a bandanna like the ones the guitar-playing hippies wore, but she didn't look anything at all like a guitar-playing hippie. She had on that little white tank top that he loved because of how it showed off the curve of her shoulders and the flatness of her tummy.

O'Henry tumbled out of the truck after him, and her smile lit up her face, and his life, and put the sun to shame…until he thought about it. The *dog* lit up her face like that? Her face was supposed to light up when she saw *him*, not his dog.

The awful possibility that Jessica didn't share his feelings, or at least not the intensity of his feelings, crossed his mind.

"Gosh, he's looking great, isn't he?" But when she glanced up at Brian, he felt instant relief. In her features he saw discovery and hope, mingled with a touch of awkwardness and confusion.

And it didn't feel as if he could ever make a mistake.

Looking at her, at the tenderness in her expression when she gazed back at him, he felt ten feet high and bulletproof.

And as a cop, he really should have known better.

"Michelle didn't come?" she asked.

"Hey, this is our date!" First the dog, then Michelle? He didn't want to share her. He wanted her all to himself. He wanted to do things with her and to her that he would barely be able to do with the dog looking on, let alone his niece.

"But the idea was for it not to feel like a date, so you could have brought her."

How many women would have the generosity of spirit that Jessica had? How many women would accept a thirteen-year-old niece as part of the deal, part of who he was now?

Besides, he reminded himself sternly, he was on his best behavior, none of his normal randy behavior would do around Jessica at all. Maybe bringing Michelle wouldn't have been such a bad idea. Built-in chaperone. Only Michelle wasn't available, because of Lucinda, who he had neglected to tell Jessica about.

"She's spending some time with her godmother." Now would be a real good time to tell her who Michelle's god-mother was. But if he wasn't willing to share this moment with his dog or his niece, how much less willing was he to spoil it by mentioning Lucinda?

"Oh, right, she told me. Aunt Lucy, right? Michelle was so thrilled that she would fly three thousand miles just to see her."

Except when he'd seen Lucinda this morning, Brian had detected a barely disguised predatory light in her eye. She hadn't come just to see Michelle. It really all seemed too complicated to explain. It could take the sparkle out of Jessica's eyes and the morning way too easily.

Jessica obviously had no idea Aunt Lucy was Lucinda Potter. Why invite the disaster he had successfully outrun so far?

They walked back to the pond together, and he stared at it. "What have you been up to?" he said, finally. A mountain of rocks had been piled where once there had just been a tiny heap.

"I just wanted to be ready to go as soon as you got here. I started hunting the property for rocks to add to the ones I'd already collected. They are not that hard to find."

He was faintly outraged that this tiny little woman had taken it upon herself to move all these rocks. Didn't she know she had a man around now?

He explained the rules. "Jessica, you're supposed to let the guy do the bull work. That's what this is for. " He tugged back his shirt sleeve and flexed a bicep for her, since she had already confessed a weakness for his arms. Her eyes fastened on that leaping muscle with a raw hunger that made his own heart beat faster. If she was going to look at him like that it was going to make it real hard to be the decent kind of guy a girl like Jessica deserved.

"I've been a woman alone for a long time," she said, then she tapped her temple. "That's what this is for."

"Brains and brawn," he said. "Perfect combination." But he was thinking of other perfect combinations, like his hardness and her softness, smothering her delicate lips with his tough ones, pulling her small frame into the embrace of his large one.

She had just said that she had been alone for a long time. It occurred to him, the thought slightly fevered, that she would have needs. He wanted to be the one to meet them. He turned his attention to the rocks, quickly.

But that moment of sizzling awareness never quite passed, and as they worked side by side, he was too aware of her. He was not sure why, but the harder she worked, the nicer she smelled. The tang of lemons and spice hung in the air around her. The fair skin on her arms darkened noticeably under the sun. Her shoulders gleamed faintly with sweat and the occasional trickle disappeared down her neck between the soft, peachlike mounds of her breasts.

But despite the fact that he was distracted and, he suspected from the occasional sidelong glance he was getting from her, so was Jessica, he was pleased to see how much they were able to accomplish and how well they worked together.

Though she was willing to do the work, she was not one of those annoying women with something to prove. There was no power struggle, no competition. She left the really heavy work to him. She didn't play any silly games about broken fingernails, and when he teasingly threw a worm he'd unearthed at her, she didn't shriek and run. She just as playfully tossed it back. This was a woman a man could take on a fishing trip!

She was the polar opposite of that woman visiting his niece and just about every other woman he had ever had anything to do with. It was refreshing. It deepened his sense that his world was being turned upside down, and it was as exhilarating and as heart-stopping as being turned upside down on any ride at the fair.

As they worked together, the conversation flowed easily between them. He updated her on O'Henry and talked of Michelle in general terms while carefully skirting the issue of the godmother.

Jessica told him about a big seed order, and some herbs

she was working with, and stopped working long enough to get his approval of the water lilies she had found for the pond.

The lilies were white, purity and sensuality mixed. He slid her a look and decided against asking her if people saw things in flowers the same way they did in inkblots.

As she chatted about her work and the small details of her life, a picture formed in his mind of her in the garden or working at her cluttered kitchen counter, content.

Contentment seemed a rare commodity these days. Unbidden, he pictured her sitting on a bench beside this pond, someday, reading a paper, the dog frolicking at her feet. And in that picture, he, Brian Kemp was right beside her, as content as she was.

It occurred to him that a word previously forbidden to him when it came to the opposite sex was beginning to link to her in his mind. The word was *future*.

He had never seen a woman work like her—unafraid to get dirty, enthused in the way she wielded the shovel. She was a woman who could be a partner in every sense of the word, though partner was another forbidden word.

Though Brian had already done most of the rough work, by noon they had completed the finishing touches on the pond hollows and they laid the heavy plastic liner down for the pond floor. She was picking through rocks as though her decisions would be life altering.

Other women would need quite a different kind of rock to put a look like that on their face, happy and reverent and totally engrossed.

"Can't we just throw them in there?" he asked, teasing.

She shook her head, and carefully continued sorting them into categories by size and color and texture. He watched the

look of concentration on her elfin face with affection, then realized he was hungry and that she apparently had no notion
you had to feed hungry men.

With a shake of his head, he hopped in his truck and
grabbed them some burgers and Cokes at a local stand and
they ate together, talking about the pond.

The truth was, except for the fact that her lips continued
to be very distracting, as did her belly button, he felt ex-
traordinarily comfortable with her. Content.

They were just finishing up lunch when O'Henry ran up
to him, something white caught fast in his teeth. He growled
playfully, daring Brian to take it from him.

"What is that?" he asked Jessica.

No answer. He looked over to see her glaring at the dog with
a look that told O'Henry she was very sorry she'd saved him.

"What?" he said again.

"Nothing," she said tersely.

Understanding dawned in him. "Has that dog got your
bloomers?"

"Never mind."

"No. No. I'll get them back for you."

"Please don't. It's not necessary. I have lots of…"

Good grief, the woman was blushing like one of her extraordinary roses. He found that hilarious. He laughed out
loud and made a grab for the dog.

"I said never mind!" she said squeakily.

He laughed again. "Hey, you're the one wearing T-shirts
advertising. Now, I've got to see them."

"No, you don't." She got up and made a grab for O'Henry,
but the wily creature lurched happily out of her grasp.

Brian stepped in front of him and got his hand on the item

in question before the dog jerked away accompanied by a faint tearing sound.

"Whoops," Brian said. But he could have saved his breath. Jessica was chasing that dog through her flowers with absolutely no consideration for what was getting wrecked. But it was Brian who was waiting when the dog burst out of the beds and onto the grass. He tackled him, but the dog, loving the game, ecstatically wriggled free, wagged his white flag at them, and charged off across the yard with Jessica hard on his heels.

The dog was amazing! He could turn in midair. He could do sudden stops and starts that would have put a quarterback to shame. He could pretend he was going left and suddenly turn right.

But just as amazing was Jessica. She had the energy of a young girl as she chased that dog. She was lithe and muscular and he loved how that little tank molded to her when she ran, how the bandanna came loose and fell free letting her wild curls escape.

Finally, she admitted defeat. She lay down on her back, panting and staring ruefully at the sky.

The dog was tiring, too. Brian made a final lunge and nearly fell over in shock when the prize came away in his fingers. The dog laid down beside Jessica and nosed under her arm looking for affection.

"Forget it," she told him. "Traitor. Benedict Arnold. Bad, bad dog."

The dog whined piteously, and her soft heart won out. She gave him a tiny little scratch on his head.

Brian came and sat, cross-legged, on the grass beside her. He could see her soft heart did not extend to him. She glared at him and held out her hand.

"Uh-uh. I won them, fair and square."

"Pervert."

He wagged his eyebrows fiendishly at her and unfolded his prize. The panties were slightly torn from the dog's teeth, plain and startlingly white. There was nothing sexy about them—no strings, no lace, no silk. They were simplicity, purity, even innocence. They reminded him of her water lilies.

For a reason he could not even fathom, he found them the sexiest underwear he had ever seen, maybe because it was all too easy to picture them hugging her slender butt, framing the tender upper portion of her thigh, caressing that cute little belly button.

"Stop it," she said, snatching them from him and squishing them into a small ball.

"Stop what?" he asked.

"Looking like that!"

"A pervert?" he suggested, fiendishly wagging his eyebrows again.

"More like an archeologist who's discovered Tut's tomb."

That's exactly how he felt. As if he had discovered unexpected treasure.

But his treasure was being wadded up and she stuffed it into the top pocket of her shorts, where they made an unsightly bulge. She looked everywhere but at him. "What do you see in the clouds?" she demanded, a clumsy effort to escape a situation that she found embarrassing and he found hilarious.

"Panties," he said, and she slugged him on his arm, hard. "Okay, water lilies."

"Oh, that's nice."

If only she knew! He rubbed his arm, and then caught her

wrist and kissed the inside of it. "I thought they were great bloomers," he told her sincerely.

"Oh, stop it. That's not what you're thinking at all. You're thinking I'm pathetic. And sexless. Old-fashioned. Ready to audition for the Little House on the Prairie fashion show. Nun-on-vacation, as your niece would say."

"You stop it," he said, and kissed the inside of her wrist again. "Any man who thought you were sexless would have to be a complete and utter moron."

She went very still beside him.

"I think," he continued, "you could be sexier in knickers than most people are in bikinis, and I mean that."

She got up on one elbow and looked at him suspiciously, and then the suspicion died. "You really do mean it."

"Sexy is about the way a woman carries herself, the way she engages life. You chasing that dog around the yard was about the sexiest thing I've ever seen."

"Get out," she said and hit his arm again, but he could tell she was pleased.

"So sexy," he said, "that I think we better take those tubes you were talking about down to the creek and cool off. Before I get ahead of myself again." His eyes fastened on her lips. He couldn't resist. He was on his best behavior, but really it was imperative he correct some of the misconceptions she entertained about herself. Just one little kiss.

That one little kiss confirmed it. Jessica was sexy without half-trying. He leaped to his feet. She was going to make it hard to be a better man.

Jessica stared at Brian wide-eyed. It was the darnedest thing. He was not kidding. He really did find her sexy, even after that stupid dog had dug right to the bottom of her undies drawer instead of picking some of those little scraps of lace and silk off the top. She had been busily collecting underwear for days now, irresistibly drawn to the lingerie shop, knowing her life was being swept in directions she had not anticipated.

Her life had not lacked anything before Brian had arrived in it, but now she was aware of the glaring holes. The most mundane things seemed fun with him. Digging a hole, putting air in tubes, chasing a dog around the yard, eating hamburgers by a pond that didn't even have water in it.

Brian Kemp was bringing her face-to-face with what she least wanted to know about herself. While her flowers bloomed gloriously, her own life had been withering away on the vine. She had been drying up from loneliness.

"I'll change into my swimsuit," she gulped.

"Bikini?" he said hopefully.

"Sorry," she said. "Same category as the bloomers." That wasn't quite true. She'd begun the job of hunting for the perfect bathing suit as soon as they'd discussed the second date.

And finally after trying on hundreds, she had settled for this one. It was plain and white, a tank style, but the cut of the leg and back showed off the slenderness of her frame and her coloring. She had bought a matching white and red rose-patterned calf-length pareu that was as sheer as gossamer. She tied it in a knot at her hip, slipped on her sandals and went out the back door.

He was sitting on the stoop and had changed into shorts. His legs were as tanned and muscular and as utterly mouth-watering as the rest of him. He had a towel slung around his neck,

He stood up and whistled softly. "Lady, you could single-handedly destroy the bikini industry."

She giggled breathlessly. She heard herself and marveled at it. She was the somber one, the serious one, the studious one. *The sexy one.* Maybe it was never too late to trade in your image for a different one. He took her hand, and she led him to the edge of the forest and a hard dirt trail that wound through the deep filtered green light of the giant cedars.

An experience that she had always delighted in—strolling down to the creek through a forest of massive cedar—felt fresh and brand-new and like the most wonderful of adventures.

But wasn't that what was happening?

Wasn't life inviting her to participate in the most wonderful adventure of all? Falling in love?

She felt the hardness of his hand in hers, and she slid him a look. Her heart felt like it had taken wing. She hadn't just been given any old guy to fall in love with, either.

No, Brian Kemp, so handsome, so assured, so funny...

Fall in love? Oh, Jessica, girl, she told herself, it's way too fast. But was it? Hadn't her heart waited for fourteen years, knowing? Believing what she had never allowed herself to believe? That he would come back?

That she would be given a second chance?

That's what he was. Brian Kemp was her second-chance man.

Her. She contemplated that word, the possessiveness of it, looked at him and tried it out again. *Her man.*

The enchantment all those years ago had been real, and it had drawn him back to her. In the end, his heart had been unable to resist what they had shared that night.

It was magical thinking, she chided herself, and yet another part of her knew that she of all people should know magic did happen. Miracles were an everyday occurrence for those who allowed themselves to see.

And wasn't love the greatest miracle of all?

Part of her felt afraid of her newfound discovery. But she was suddenly aware that fear had held her back for too long. Her life had been fine, but had it had this sparkle? Had the very air shimmered around her with promise?

No, no it hadn't because when it came to love she had been ruled by suspicion and fear. She had settled for a half life.

But now she decided, firmly, being hurt would be better than going through life half alive. She didn't want to miss all that was best, or be removed from all the color and vibrancy and total intensity of sensation by the veil of mistrust.

Her hand tightened in his.

And a voice inside her whispered, believe. Believe in that light that you give so generously and readily to others. Believe.

He glanced down at his hand, a surprised look on his face. "Woman," he said, "you make me tingle."

Woman. Not a girl, anymore. So ready. This time, so right.

"You make me tingle, too."

And then she was running down the path in front of him, her tube over her shoulder, breathless with laughter and hope, feeling as alive as when she was a child. With a whoop of pure delight she came around the final twist in the trail, and the creek gurgled before her. She heard him behind her, untied the pareu, and let it drop. She heard his appreciative gasp, turned to wink at him, and then leaped in.

Just as she was doing with her life. And it felt this wonderful: the cold and invigorating water bringing her awake, as if she had been half-asleep before.

She turned back to see Brian standing on the bank, grinning.

"It's even better wet," he told her.

"Life?" she asked him, still swimming in the glory of her discoveries.

"The bathing suit."

"Oh!" She splashed at him, but he artfully dodged out of her way.

"Is that as cold as it looks?"

"Colder!" she said, ecstatically. "Get in! It's wonderful."

He stuck his toe in, pulled it back out, wrinkled his nose.

She laughed out loud, because she would have thought he would be the bold one. But love was making her bold, and she hopped back out of the water and chased him around the glen until she had hold of him and then she pushed and pulled until she had him at the water's edge.

He set himself like a rock, allowing her to amuse him by trying to get him into the water. Then, way too easily, he scooped her up in his arms and waded out into the creek.

His eyes took in every inch of her, and just when she thought he was going to kiss her, he dropped her back into the cold pool!

She came out sputtering, then linked her arms like she was going to swing a baseball bat, and hit the surface. A wall of water cascaded over him. She barely had time to appreciate the wonder of that gorgeous male body soaked, when he came at her, his palms thrusting the water at her in gigantic splashes. It was war! They played until they were both soaked and nearly hysterical from laughing. The glade rang with the merriment of their shouts and screams and the happy yelps of O'Henry.

Finally, exhausted, they retrieved the tubes. They each climbed on, butts in the holes, limbs draped over the sides, and turned their faces to the sun. Hands linked, they let the lazy current take them. They drifted down the creek talking about nothing and everything, laughing at what they saw in the clouds and at the fish that sometimes grew bold enough to nibble their toes. O'Henry swam beside them and explored the banks and appeared to luxuriate in their happiness, as though it was radiating outward from them.

And then that sense of excitement and energy built in her again, and she slipped out of her tube, came up underneath his and gave it a mighty butt. The tube capsized, sending him into the water. They were in a deep hole, the water tranquil and blue.

They swam together, ducking and splashing and laughing, until without warning she found herself locked in Brian's embrace. Her wet, slick body pressed against his as he held her tight with one arm and treaded water with the other.

He felt wonderful, his skin cool and slippery and sensuous. His lips captured hers and his free hand tangled in the wet strands of her curls, allowing her no escape.

Not that escaping was on her mind. Jessica met his kiss, playfully at first, but then they were very much a man and a woman.

"We're going to drown," she said breathlessly.

"What a way to go," he said and deepened the kiss. Their heads submerged under the water, but their lips remained locked, his arms strong around her.

Seconds later they burst to the surface, gasping.

"Is this your idea of going slow?" she asked.

"It's kind of getting away from me," he admitted, grinning boyishly.

"Brian?"

"Uh-huh?"

She pressed her wet curves into him so tightly that it felt like they were heating the cool water around them, melting together. "I'm tired of going slow."

"Jessica?"

"Uh-huh?"

"Me, too."

She was going to seduce him. It was as easy as that. Of course, she had never done anything quite like a seduction before, so it amazed her how easily it came to her.

"My place," she said.

They moved from the water and soon were chasing each other back down the forest path, stopping to share breathless giggles and touch each other daringly, to kiss. His hand found her breast, touched with gentle reverence, and then they were running again.

They broke, finally, into the clearing by her cottage.

"I had no idea we had drifted that far down the creek," he said. "Did it take forever to get back here?"

"Fourteen years," she said.

"Forever," he said.

They ran across her lawn, and she burst through the back door of her cottage, Brian's hand in hers.

And skidded to a halt.

Michelle sat there facing the door, fresh-cut flowers scattered around her, her tongue caught between her teeth as she sorted them into careful bundles.

Sitting across from her, her back to the door was a

woman whose black hair flowed like a rich dark waterfall down her back.

"Uncle Brian! Where have you been? Your station called. I thought when I couldn't get you on the phone, you'd be outside working on the pond, but you weren't. We decided to wait for you. Whoever phoned said it was an emergency."

Jessica's wet skin, which had felt so heated, suddenly felt cold as ice, and not because of a police emergency. She dropped Brian's hand.

The woman turned. "Hello, Brian," she said softly.

Her eyes drifted to Jessica. None of the shocked recognition that Jessica felt could be seen in the woman's eyes.

They were as beautiful as sapphires and just as cold. The sooty, thick lashes closed over them as she squinted narrowly, assessingly at Jessica.

Lucinda Potter.

Jessica felt like she had walked out of the most delicious dream and landed in a complete nightmare.

Brian swore softly, then sighed, a man apparently resigned to having things go wrong. "Jessica, do you remember Lucinda?"

Chapter Eight

Brian wasn't sure what kind of problem they were having at work, but he was pretty sure it couldn't compete with the one he found himself in here. If someone had handed him a pen and told him to create his worst nightmare, he couldn't have done the bang-up job that was now in Jessica's crowded little kitchen.

Jessica had let go of his hand as if it scorched her, as if he had turned into a fire-breathing monster in less time than it took to draw a full breath in and out. He tried to catch her eye, but she had taken a sudden interest in that scrap of enticing film she had around her waist and was fiddling with the knot at her hip.

On the other hand, Lucinda was looking at him with the half-lidded gaze he had always thought was supremely sexy, her head tucked to one side, a faint smile playing across red lips.

Only now the look wasn't the least sexy. It seemed faintly contrived and silly. After a man had seen plain white bloomers, could he ever go back?

No doubt Jessica had not missed a single nuance of that look Lucinda was giving him.

He sighed. He couldn't contemplate this under pressure. He knew he would not have received a call from work unless it was of grave importance.

"Can I use your phone?" he asked.

Jessica nodded curtly toward the phone that hung on the wall. He tried to connect with her on the way over there, but she turned her back on him and let O'Henry in the house. His quick glimpse of her eyes showed they had completely lost their animation. The gold of the sun seemed to be draining from her skin. She looked white and shaken.

He was causing her pain without half-trying. He didn't find disaster, it found him. Why had he ever entertained the notion that he and Jessica might be a good combination? Lucy was probably more his type, a woman harder to hurt than a rhino, though better looking.

"You don't have to call in," Lucinda told him, breezily. "I'm only here for a few days, after all. You could pretend you never got the message."

Actually, he couldn't do that, and he was annoyed at Lucinda for suggesting it in front of Michelle. He slid another look at Jessica, who was still engrossed in the dog. She was a woman incapable of pretense or telling lies to get her own way.

"I certainly wouldn't want to let some civic disaster spoil your plans, Lucinda" he said sarcastically.

Lucinda's smile widened. "My thoughts exactly."

He realized that he'd inadvertently made it sound like he would go along with Lucinda's plans, if she had any. He was terrible at walking this kind of tightrope. He shot Jessica another look.

She was scratching the dog's ears so vigorously he wanted to warn her she might detach them from O'Henry's head. But then she might be embarrassed, and he didn't want to embarrass her in front of Lucinda. He had enough damage control to do already.

"I have to change," Jessica mumbled suddenly and slid out of the room with the dog behind her.

He wanted to go after her. Maybe she guessed, because he heard the bolt slide shut on the bathroom door. He debated going after her anyway, but then picked up the phone.

"I told you he'd call," Michelle said to her aunt and sighed.

As it turned out, the problem at work did rival the one here. A high-speed chase had turned bad when the fugitive had hit a pump at a gas station. Fuel was flying everywhere and the perpetrator was now holed up inside the station, threatening to shoot anyone who moved. Apparently that included anyone who tried to turn off the fuel. It was at one of the busiest intersections in town. Roads were being closed. Nearby residences and businesses had been evacuated. There was a church behind the service station that had been hosting its youth group when the crisis started. There were thirty-three kids trapped inside, caught between a mad gunman and the possibility of an explosion.

Every available man was being called in. To contain the crisis, to help evacuations, to direct traffic. He heard the unspoken. *Or to mop up.*

Brian had zero time to do anything about the situation

here. At least, as far as he could tell, the situation with Jessica and Lucy was not life threatening.

"I've got to go," he said tersely as he set down the phone. "Thanks for coming out here to bring the message, Michelle. You did the right thing."

Okay, there were consequences he hadn't even begun to sort through, but it was still the right thing.

"How come you have to go to work, Unkie?" Michelle asked, concern etched in her features. She was wearing makeup again today, expertly applied. He thought it made her look too old. And the clothes were just a little too racy for a thirteen-year-old. He'd have to talk to her about it. Or Lucinda.

But that wasn't his priority right now. His priority was to protect her. "It's just a little accident."

"No, it isn't," Michelle said. "They wouldn't be calling you to work on your day off if it was. Uncle Brian, don't go."

"Yeah," Lucinda echoed and batted her lashes at him. "Don't go."

He shot her a look that he hoped she correctly interrupted as murderous. Apparently murder was just as appealing to her as other things. She licked her lips and tossed her heavy mane of hair over her shoulder.

Unfortunately, Lucinda was doing her impression of a mafia moll just as Jessica reentered the room, the bathing suit replaced with a pale peach pantsuit that looked like something his dental hygienist wore.

"I have to go," he told her.

He looked around the room. This was some kind of record, even for him. Michelle looked furiously, unforgivingly angry. Lucinda looked insulted. And Jessica looked…heartbroken.

He took her by her elbow, felt her resistance, but had no time to be gentle. He forced her out the back door with him. "Look, I'm sorry. I don't have time to explain about her being here."

"You don't owe me any explanations."

She was trying hard to be proud and to act like it didn't matter that he hadn't told her about Lucinda.

"Listen to me." As quickly as he could he told her about the crisis unfolding.

Worry, intense and forceful, filled her eyes and clouded her expression, and then she quickly masked it.

"There's no controlling Lucinda, but try not to let Michelle watch TV," he said in a low tone. Apparently the fact that he was familiar enough with Lucinda to know she was uncontrollable was not a point in his favor, but he bulldozed ahead.

"And if you can keep them from leaving that would be good, too. They'll turn on the radio as soon as they get in the car. Or run into a roadblock and find out."

"You want me to entertain your ex-girlfriend?"

He wanted to protest that Lucinda was not his ex-girlfriend, but of course she was, and the memories of those intimacies shared in a moment of grief just months ago were flaring a little too brightly in Lucinda's eyes.

Okay, he had some fires to put out in his personal life. Big ones. But, this time, the ones in his professional life had to come first. He was better at those, anyway.

He felt an urgent need to kiss Jessica—as if that would explain all the things he had no time and no words to explain. But when he leaned toward her she ducked under his arm and went back through the door.

"Trust me," he called softly after her.

She turned and looked at him, her eyes huge and pain-filled. He suspected he'd used up his get-out-of-jail-free card with Jessica a long, long time ago. The door slapped shut behind her with what seemed to be cold finality.

He turned and ran for his truck.

Jessica leaned against the door, her head spinning. She had come within a hair of throwing caution to the wind, caving in to the spell of enchantment that had been building around her for weeks, and making love with Brian Kemp.

It was insanely out of character for her. And the sad truth was that nothing short of a disaster could have stopped her.

So, the universe had stepped in and provided one.

Two, actually. The one unfolding downtown—her heart beat crazily with fear at the thought of him going there—and the other one, Lucinda Potter, sitting at Jessica's kitchen table, looking wildly out of place in her silk designer suit.

Lucinda Potter was in her kitchen. She was Michelle's godmother and somehow Brian had neglected to let Jessica know that little detail.

And before she'd had a chance to bring him to task for it, he'd been called out on a mission that sounded horribly dangerous.

How could you be so killingly angry at a man who's life was in danger? At a man who was about to risk it all in service to his fellow citizens?

If she had tried to invent a nightmare she couldn't have done nearly this well for herself.

Jessica had always been able to put Michelle first, and she told herself that was what she was going to have to do now. She had to set aside her personal feelings and do as Brian had asked. She would set aside the desire to go into her bedroom, lock the door and intermittently nurse heartbreak and worry. She could do that tomorrow. Tonight, she had to try and keep Michelle from the TV set or the news on the radio, even if that meant keeping Lucinda in her house.

Of course, she had no idea how to do that. It was obvious the intervening years had changed very little about Lucinda. They would have nothing in common. How was she going to keep her here? Talk about horticulture? Lucinda looked like she would be entertained by that for about three seconds.

Feeling like a warrior about to do battle, Jessica marched back into her kitchen, her chin tilted high. "Tea, anyone?"

Lucinda snorted.

Off to a good start, Jessica thought. "Would you like anything else, then?"

"Have you got anything stronger than tea?"

In a moment of blinding inspiration, Jessica knew exactly how she was going to keep Lucinda here.

"Why yes, I do," she said innocently. Jessica went down to the cellar to retrieve her aunt's bootleg homemade peach brandy—probably the strongest liquor a person could consume without inviting blindness. But Hetty's brew didn't taste as if it had that kind of power. No, it tasted light and fruity, as innocent as drinking a glass of wine, but it kicked like a mule.

As she brushed dust off the bottle, Michelle was making frantic cutting motions with her hands behind Lucinda's back. Jessica ignored her and poured Lucinda a tumbler of Aunt Hetty's home brew. A tumbler was generally enough to knock a logger or a longshoreman right off his feet. It should be plenty to keep Lucinda from heading for town or turning on her car radio.

Lucinda eyed the glass with distaste, and then took a cautious little sip. Her eyes widened appreciatively.

"My, isn't that tasty?" Lucinda said, smacking her lips. "Amazing. Did you make it yourself?"

Jessica sensed, for the first time, she had some value to Lucinda. "It's an old family recipe."

"Delicious." Lucinda took another drink.

Michelle glowered at Jessica. "Were you holding Uncle Brian's hand when you came in the door?" she asked. Apparently it was tit for tat—if Jessica was going to make her life miserable by ignoring her warnings about serving her godmother alcohol, Michelle was going to fire back.

"Holding his hand?" Lucinda asked, her eyes widening. Her back had been to the door when Jessica and Brian had come in. She looked at Jessica in a brand-new way and took another slug of her drink, her eyes narrow.

"We weren't really holding hands," Jessica said. She was not used to telling lies, and she could feel her nose starting to burn. She was not going to have her humiliating heartbreak exposed to this woman. "I had slipped coming up the stairs. He reached out to steady me."

Michelle looked skeptical. "It looked like you'd been laughing. Really hard. Unless your face was flushed from something else."

"No, from laughing! Sometimes people do that when they fall. Try to see the humor in it, laugh it off to cover how embarrassed they are."

"Something else?" Lucinda said, suspiciously. Her eyes raked Jessica and then dismissed her. "Frankly, you don't look like Brian's type. He likes his women a touch flashier."

"You should have seen Bambi," Michelle muttered.

"Who?" Lucinda asked, her interest more than just casual.

"Never mind," Michelle said.

Lucinda apparently decided to focus on the known opponent.

Though Jessica was well aware she had not been much of an opponent many years ago, and she made even less of one now. They didn't even come from the same world. Lucinda was slick and sophisticated and beautiful in the most glamorous sense of the word. She probably never had dirt under her fingernails or spiders on her pillowcase.

The question was, which world did Brian truly belong in? *Mine,* Jessica thought. But that didn't mean he would choose it. He hadn't last time.

"How did you come to know Brian? And my godchild? When he introduced us, didn't he ask if you remembered me?"

"Uncle Brian knew Jessica from high school."

Jessica felt like she was a bug that had been placed under a microscope. Lucinda narrowed her eyes, took a long thoughtful draw on her drink, and studied Jessica.

"High school?" Lucinda said at length. "No, I don't think so. Jessica? I'm sure I didn't know anyone by that name."

To be remembered would not have been as humiliating as being completely forgotten. Those small cruelties and slights had not even been aimed at her personally.

"No," Jessica said firmly. "We did not know each other."

"Jessica was a geek," Michelle filled in helpfully.

"Oh," Lucinda said. "That explains it." She giggled, and Jessica realized she had already consumed nearly half that tumbler of brandy. "Michelle, did I ever tell you about the time your mother and I went into the boy's washroom? We pretended we were holding a survey. It was hysterical."

Both Michelle and Jessica waited for her to tell them the

hysterical part, but apparently she thought it was self-evident. She drank deeply from her brandy, then launched into another high school memory. She ended with "Amanda was just the best, wasn't she, Michelle?"

"The best," Michelle echoed, but something in her tone made Jessica shoot her a worried look. Michelle seemed terribly remote, as if she was looking at her godmother from behind a wall of glass.

"Brian and I dated in high school," Lucinda said. "Did you know that?"

"Yes, I did," Jessica said glumly.

"I didn't," Michelle said, and some of the remoteness left her face. Her brows scrunched up.

"We almost got married once." Lucinda sighed. "Did you know that?"

"No, I didn't." Jessica refrained from adding she could have lived long and happily without knowing it, too.

"I didn't, either," Michelle said, and her brows scrunched up even more. "Why didn't he tell me that?"

"Darling, don't do that with your face. You'll get premature furrows. Yes, not marrying Brian was one of my mistakes," Lucinda said, as if neither of them had spoken. She contemplated her drink, sipped, then sipped again. "This is *really* good. I wanted him to be a lawyer, like Kevin. He wasn't about to be convinced, so I followed Kevin and Amanda out to Toronto and eventually met and married the lawyer I dreamed of."

She took another long, measured sip of the drink. "Another of my mistakes," she said. That ended in a hiccup.

Michelle sent Jessica a baleful look.

"Michelle," Jessica said quickly into the silence, hoping

to cut off Lucinda before she got anymore personal. "How are the flower arrangements going? Are you putting together some orders?"

Michelle, who had been bundling flowers shoved them aside, knit her hands together and gave Jessica a dark look. "My aunt and I were supposed to go shopping," she said. "I doubt if we'll be going now."

"Nonsense, silly girl. I'll just finish my drink, and we'll be on our way."

Jessica knew nobody finished a tumbler of Auntie's brew and went on their way, but how did Michelle know?

"Those are the cutest flower arrangements you've got Michelle making," Lucinda said. "In fact, this is just the cutest place I've ever seen. Adorable."

Though she was smiling as she said it, Jessica could hear that Lucinda thought cute and adorable rated right up there with boring and monotonous.

"Thank you."

"I'm sorry. Did you tell me how you reconnected with Brian?" Lucinda asked.

"No, I didn't," Jessica said. And she wasn't going to, either. Her and Brian's relationship was private. Up until a few minutes ago, she might have even said sacred. It was not something she would allow Lucinda to put under her microscope.

"I'm going to feed O'Henry," Michelle said suddenly, getting up from the table. Some of the flowers fell on the floor. She ignored them. "Why don't you come with me, Jessica?"

O'Henry's food was not outside, but nevertheless Jessica followed Michelle out the back door.

"I didn't know about her and Uncle Brian," Michelle said,

worried, but still angry, too. "Do you think that's why she's here? Do you think she wants him back?"

There was something very close to panic in the young girl's voice.

"I don't know," Jessica said, trying for a soothing note, though Michelle had just articulated her own deepest fear.

"Why did you do that?" Michelle demanded, her voice shrill and querulous.

"What?"

"Give her a drink!"

"She asked for one," Jessica reminded the girl.

"Well, she can never have just one. Just like my mother." The statement was loaded with fury. In the silence that followed, Michelle seemed to realize what she had said. She looked aghast. "I didn't mean it to sound like that."

Jessica wondered if there was any other way it could sound. "It's okay, sweetheart. I'm sure your mom was only human. She probably had a few flaws, just like the rest of us."

"She didn't! My mother was the best. She was!"

The child bit down hard on her fist, as if she could smother the pain in her heart with the physical pain her teeth were inflicting on her tender skin.

Jessica reached for her, but Michelle dodged out of the way, called her dog and ran off into the flower beds.

Jessica watched her go, saw her sit on a bench, and draw the puppy into her arms. She knew Michelle was crying into his fur. As much as she wanted to go to her, she knew there were times when it was better to leave things alone. Jessica reluctantly went back through the door into her kitchen.

Lucinda had emptied the tumbler and refilled it. She had made rather startling headway into the second glass. Her lipstick was starting to slide off her lips and her eyes looked faintly crossed. She had picked up a flower off the table and stuffed it behind her ear.

Jessica tried to feel ashamed of herself.

"She's a funny little mite, isn't she?" Lucinda asked, leaning forward confidentially, the flower bobbing wildly. "It's my duty as her mother, I mean her godmother, to help her. Somebody has got to show the poor little thing how to dress."

She went into a long and rambling resume about what qualified her as a fashion consultant to a thirteen-year-old.

By the time she was done, so was the second tumbler of brandy.

She reached for the bottle, and so did Jessica, but Lucinda was a little quicker. "Just one more little sip," she said, the words slurred almost beyond recognition. She poured another glass to the rim.

Jessica was not sure she wanted to be responsible for a person who had drank three tumblers of Aunt Hetty's brandy.

"I'm not sure that's such a good idea."

"Look, you little mouse…" this was followed by a series of drunken snickers. "How about if you don't tell me what's a good idea?"

"All right," Jessica conceded and folded her arms over her chest. *Little mouse.* She'd happily provide Lucinda with another bottle, since this one was now done. Not that a living soul had ever managed to get into a second bottle of Hetty's Peach Ambrosia.

On a different level, she wondered if Brian would share Lucinda's view of her. See her as a little mouse. He hadn't acted like he'd been chasing a mouse up the forest path, earlier.

But then Jessica had a limited understanding of men and their motivations, and where Brian was concerned she was far too willing to paint him with a golden-edged brush.

"I'll tell you what's a good idea," Lucinda blurted out, very loudly. "A good idea would be for me and Brian to try it again. That child needs a mother. Who better than me? I'm already her godmother. I was her mother's best friend. Brian and I have always had a spark. Always." Each loud word was very carefully enunciated.

"You don't think you have a chance with him, do you?" Lucinda asked, her lips curling cruelly.

"I hadn't thought about it," Jessica lied.

"That's good." Without warning Lucinda's eyes filled up with tears. They spilled over and half her lashes washed down her cheeks.

"I let him get away," she wailed. "I can't believe I let him slip away."

And then her eyes closed. Without warning her body went limp and her head fell down on the table. Her hand was still curled possessively around Hetty's brandy. When Jessica tried to take the brandy away, her grip tightened on it, and she mumbled, "I won't let him get away this time. Oh, no, I have not begun…"

The sentence ended abruptly in a snore. It looked like Lucinda was going to slide right onto the floor. Jessica managed to stop her descent and then somehow wrestle the limp body to the couch. She had pulled off Lucinda's shoes and covered her lightly with the crocheted throw she kept there.

Jessica went to the window. Michelle and the dog were laying on the grass, now, staring up at the stars that were starting to wink in a velvet sky.

Jessica, never taking her eyes off the young girl, switched on the radio. The news was live at the scene. The gas pumps had been shut off, and the children evacuated from the church. There was no mention whether anyone had been hurt, but the newscaster reminded his audience that the night was far from over.

Jessica watched Michelle sit up, stretch, climb to her feet and amble toward the house. Reluctantly, she turned the radio back off.

"Where's Aunt Lucy?" she asked, looking at the lipstick-smudged tumbler on the table with disgust.

"She's, er, having a little sleep."

"I tried to tell you," Michelle said, woefully, after glancing briefly in at her aunt who was sprawled out on the couch.

"You did try to tell me," Jessica said. "I'm sorry." Not sorry enough so that she didn't consider doing the same thing to Michelle so she could turn on the TV and find out what was happening with Brian.

She recognized how desperate that was. With every bit of discipline she possessed, she reached over and ruffed Michelle's hair.

"Do you need to talk?"

"No."

"Okay, then, how about some Scrabble?"

Michelle looked at her stiffly, but then capitulated. "Oh, okay," she said with ill grace.

They played Scrabble until nearly midnight. Lucinda showed no sign of stirring, not that Jessica would have let her drive anyway.

"I've got to go to bed," Michelle finally said. "Do you suppose Uncle Brian's all right?"

"He's fine, sweetie."

"Are you guessing, or do you have the inside track?"

"I feel as if I would know if something had happened to him."

"Me, too," Michelle decided. She gathered up her dog and trundled off to the bedroom she was slowly making into her own.

Jessica waited as long as was humanly possible before she tiptoed in and checked on the child. And then she went right to the TV.

She shoved Lucinda's feet out of the way and sat down on the couch.

She turned on the TV just in time to catch the end of the special coverage. The crisis was over. One policeman had been seriously wounded when shots were fired.

Her breath caught in her throat. What nonsense that she would *know* if something had happened to him. Why would she?

It was not as if she had been right about one single thing about him so far. She hugged her knees to her. What was true about Brian? Sometimes she felt she knew, beyond the shadow of a doubt, and other times *all* she knew was shadowed with doubt.

She knew she loved him. She just didn't know if that was complete folly.

The phone jangled, and she leaped up, raced to the kitchen and grabbed the receiver off the wall. "Yes?"

"It wasn't me, Jessica. I'm fine."

His voice was deep and rough. She closed her eyes and let it sink into her, let herself fill slowly with a most wondrous gratitude.

He'd known she would be sitting here, watching the news. He'd known. He probably knew how hopeless and helpless she was where he was concerned.

"Is Michelle okay?" he asked.

"She's sleeping. I managed to keep them here. She doesn't even know what happened."

"Thanks, Jessica."

Tell him Lucinda—the woman he almost married—is passed out like a drunken trollop on the couch.

But she didn't. Her voice a whisper, before she weakened and confessed every secret of her heart to him, she said, "Good night, Brian." And she didn't wait to see what he answered before she hung up.

She'd hung up on him. Brian did not think that was a good thing. Nope, he was sure he was in terrible trouble. It wasn't enough that he hadn't told her about Lucinda. Nope, then he'd left Lucy with Jessica.

He wasn't sure how you went about fixing something like this, but his tired mind insisted on debating it anyway.

He'd flubbed up in a grand way. He had to let Jessica know Lucinda was nothing to him.

He had to let her know the truth. That was what she'd advised him at the beginning. Tell the truth.

The truth was that he loved her.

Should he call her back? What if she hung up on him again? What if she was trying to sleep?

The truth: sometime tonight, in that terrible moment when those shots had rung out and Lance had fallen beside him, Brian had prepared himself to die. One regret had stung him. That he had not given his life to someone like Jessica a long time ago. That he had wasted so much time living in a place of gray and black but no color, a place that had sound but no music.

He felt a sharp and surprising regret that he would have made love to her this afternoon without committing to her. That would have been so wrong.

Maybe it was a good thing fate had intervened and made him realize, if he survived, what he really wanted for his life. It wasn't one more fling, that was for sure.

And when he had survived, he'd realized maybe it wasn't too late.

For once in his life, he wasn't going to walk away from a woman he'd disappointed. He was going to ask her forgiveness. He was going to do everything in his power to make things right between him and Jessica.

He rehearsed what to say, but nothing seemed to be right.

And then he had it! He was terrible with words. They wouldn't be big enough, anyway, to make her understand that he knew how colossally stupid he had been.

What about a grander gesture? Him getting down on one knee and declaring himself? Asking her, Jessica Moran, to walk the days of her life with him, Brian Kemp?

He pictured opening a ring box, presenting it to her, the startled look on her face, the happiness, the tears of joy forming in her eyes.

A ring, he realized, wearily. He just needed a ring.

And with that thought on his mind, he finally took off his uniform, climbed between his sheets, and fell into the most peaceful sleep he had experienced in weeks.

Chapter Nine

Brian awoke and knew immediately something was different. He noticed the sun streaming in his window, the riotous birdsong outside.

He realized he was happy.

He was a man with a plan, a purpose, a mission. Plus, he was in love. He thought of Jessica and smiled, remembering how she had looked in that bathing suit, the taste of her lips, the look in her eyes. He had some work to do to get things back on track, but he was pretty sure the surprise he had planned for her was just the ticket.

He leaped from bed, whistling. He had a lot to do today. It might be the most important day of his life. He could not blow it.

He showered, debated what to wear. Doctor-going-golfing for this special occasion? No, Jessica liked him fine just the way he was. At least she had until yesterday. And once he put things right, she would again. He pulled on a T-shirt and a pair of jeans and heard the front door open.

Michelle was coming in, Lucinda trailing behind her. Lucinda wore dark glasses and looked a little piqued.

"I heard about it on the radio coming from Jessica's," Michelle said, without even saying hello. She crossed her arms and tapped her foot. "A little accident? Half the city could have been blown up. You could have been killed!"

The man he was yesterday might have argued with her. The man he had been yesterday might have tried to convince her.

The man he was today led with his heart.

"But I wasn't," he said, and then he lunged at his surprised niece, picked her up under the arms and swung her over his head like he had done when she was a little girl. And just as he had then, she began to shriek with laughter.

"A little less noise, puh-leese," Lucinda said, wincing, and placed tapered fingers to her temples.

"She drank too much last night," Michelle tattled with vicious enjoyment after Brian had set her back on the floor.

"Your little friend got me plastered," Lucinda said to Brian. "Who would have thought, to look at her, she'd be capable of that?"

He found it faintly amusing that Lucinda wanted to blame her liquor consumption on someone else, especially someone like Jessica who looked as if she drank a glass of wine maybe three or four times a year.

Lucinda looked miffed that he hadn't agreed with her, that he obviously wasn't nearly as ready to pawn off her behavior on someone else as she was. Grouchily, she said, "The stuff she's got in her basement probably isn't even legal. You should check her out."

"Oh, I plan to," he said, deadpan. Boy, did he plan to check Jessica out. In every room possible, too. In the kitchen and bathroom and basement and out in the garden.

Lucinda cocked an eyebrow at him. "What did I detect in that little statement?"

He realized he had to go to Jessica with a completely clean slate. And that meant everybody had to be on the same page. His past had to be completely cleared up and laid to rest and everyone had to know it.

"Come on, Lucy, I'll buy you lunch." She had always hated it when he called her Lucy, but suddenly that's what she reminded him of. Lucy of Charlie Brown fame, that self-assured girl who always put her own interests first. It was time to tell her. It was not going anywhere between them. It was never going anywhere. And then he'd be completely free.

To go to Jessica and declare himself.

"Can I come for lunch?" Michelle asked, looking from him to Lucinda and back again, her brows knit anxiously.

"Not this time," he said. "Tell you what, though, Lucinda and I will go to eat at that new place in the mall, and you can meet some of your friends for a burger or something."

Michelle did not look mollified.

Lucinda wrinkled her nose. "A mall restaurant?"

He wasn't prepared to pay Smuggler's Lair prices to break bad news to her. She probably wasn't going to eat her lunch, anyway. If she was the same Lucinda she'd always been there was a good chance he was going to end up wearing whatever she ordered.

Because all her life Lucinda had gotten what Lucinda wanted. Only this time what she wanted was him, and he was taken.

Taken.

Taken by a woman who was sweetness and light and honesty. Taken by a woman who loved simple things and would never care if it was a mall restaurant.

He had a sudden moment of doubt. What if Jessica said no? What made him think he deserved a woman like that? Had anything in her face yesterday encouraged him to believe she would say yes? She had hung up on him last night.

But he shook off the doubt. Of course she wouldn't say no! Not after he straightened everything out. Jessica had a gift for seeing, and he just knew she had always seen what was best in him. Maybe even before it had existed.

Michelle went and made a phone call. "I'm going to hang out with my friends this afternoon, but I'll meet them at the mall." She was still miffed about being excluded from the lunch invitation.

"That's wonderful, darling," Lucinda said absently. "Your uncle and I have some adult business to look after. Very adult."

Michelle looked even more sullen at that announcement. She rolled her eyes, and then they went out to the truck. Lucinda's rented BMW was parked behind it.

Lucinda surveyed the truck. "Really, Brian, what were you thinking with that color? Don't you think it's time for something a little more refined? It's got to be ten years older than I am."

"Ancient," Michelle muttered, which earned her a sour look from her godmother.

Brian laughed. He was taken by a woman who loved ancient orange trucks.

"How about if I just follow you?" he suggested. Then he wouldn't have to drive her back. Then he could lose no time in selecting a ring and heading out to Jessica's.

Half an hour later he watched through the restaurant window as Michelle met with her friends. Lucinda was studying the menu. The selection was not meeting with her approval. She put in a special order for a salad, adding and deleting items from the order twice, apparently unaware of the look of black annoyance she was receiving from the waitress.

Brian was taken by a woman who would be happy with the house special, a smothered hamburger. One who would have named the flower the waitress was wearing over her ear and asked the woman where she'd gotten it.

Lucinda slid off her sunglasses. Michelle had been right. She looked ancient.

"I guess I look like hell."

She did, actually. Ancient, tired, and hard.

Thankfully, she did not wait for an answer. Her hand covered his. "Brian, I think we both have to think about what's best for Michelle."

He frowned. Best for Michelle? "What do you mean? Doesn't she seem like a happy, well-adjusted thirteen-year-old?" *Especially now?* In the past few weeks his niece had blossomed under Jessica's tender loving care. And so had he.

Lucinda sighed and patted his hand patiently. "She needs a mother, a feminine influence in her life."

He had not gotten around to thinking about how good his decision to marry Jessica was going to be for Michelle. But what Lucinda was saying was so true! Jessica would be a wonderful mother figure to his niece. She could teach Michelle what it was to be a woman, a real woman, not the way magazines portrayed them at all. A woman who was nice to waitresses, who knew the value of an old truck, who didn't mind dog hair, and who knew how to enjoy a hot summer afternoon on the creek.

"I think the choice is obvious," Lucinda continued.

So did he!

"And it's me."

His mouth fell open even as he realized he should have seen this coming, probably would have if he was not so preoccupied with his own thoughts.

"We should have done this years ago," she said.

He stared at her absolutely flabbergasted. "We thought of doing this years ago," he reminded her. "You didn't want to spend your life with a cop."

He suddenly felt so grateful that he had taken a different road, one that had made him the kind of man that might have a chance with Jessica. A road that had led him back to her.

"I know I had my chance once," Lucinda said, pouting prettily. "But I knew, after the funeral, you'd forgiven me for that particular lapse in judgement. And we're both still young, Brian. Making up for lost time should be fun."

This shouldn't surprise him. This is what she had meant when she told Michelle they had adult business to discuss. And from the look in her eye, she intended to cement her suggestion in a very adult way.

That was what they were here to straighten out, once and for all.

"We're going to be great together," she said, leaning toward him, giving him a nice view of her rather remarkable décolleté. "A wonderful team. Of course, I have no interest in any additional family, besides Michelle. Babies, frankly, are horrible. Thankfully, you have never struck me as the daddy type."

He hadn't thought of the union between he and Jessica in quite those terms yet, but suddenly he did. He felt like he could, indeed, be the daddy type. In fact, the thought filled him with a bubbling sense of joy. He was going to be the father to Jessica's children. And she'd want children. He just knew it. Probably at least three.

The years they had ahead of them! First teeth and first steps. Santa Claus and the Easter bunny. Was her little acreage big enough for a pony? He thought her place would be better than his for the kids. Big enough to play ball.

"I should have said yes all those years ago," Lucinda said, completely oblivious to the fact that he was barely at the table with her, his mind taking him to some happy place in the future. "I shouldn't have run out on you. It was a terrible mistake."

He came to his senses. He snatched his hand out from under hers. There were probably delicate ways to phrase what he had to say, but he couldn't think of one. All he could think of was telling the truth, and quickly. "Lucinda, we are not going to be together. Not in that way, not ever."

Not even if Jessica said no. He would never be able to settle for the Lucindas of the world, now.

Jessica had ruined him.

Or resurrected him, depending on how he looked at it.

"You don't want to marry me?" she asked, stunned. She was so sure, even now, of her power over men, so sure she could have whatever she wanted.

"No. Not now. Not ever."

Her mouth pursed, and she sat back, glaring at him.

"Please don't throw your salad on me."

She set it down with effort. "As if I would," she said haughtily. "I only suggested you and me because I thought it would be best for Michelle."

He knew she was saving her pride. Michelle had probably only figured remotely into Lucinda's equation.

Still, he played along with her. "What Michelle needs is to see two people really in love, secure enough in themselves that they can give her everything." He was amazed those words had come out of his own mouth.

"You sound as if you have someone in mind."

"Yes."

"Not this Bambi that Michelle has mentioned with such derision?"

"You don't know the first thing about me, do you?" he asked quietly, surprised.

"I thought I did." She studied him intently, then her eyes widened with horrified disbelief. "Oh, no! Please don't tell me you've fallen for that little mouse out at Snow White's cabin. Really, Brian!"

Little mouse? His Jessica? He felt like he was going to throw something, but looking at her, he was reminded that Lucinda didn't know the true value of anything. She was so engrossed in image, she managed to miss the essence over and over again.

The anger left him. He suddenly felt very sorry for Lucinda. "I'm going to marry Jessica," he said firmly.

Lucinda stared at him. "My God, you are not kidding." She shook her head in disbelief, toyed with her salad, and then laid down her fork. "Let's just go, shall we? You've managed to spoil lunch entirely."

All his life he had felt the weight of people expecting him to make them happy. They had made him feel unbearably selfish when he had not met their needs. Now he saw a most unexpected lesson about his life. He had remained strong in his own truth, even though it had cost him. He had not allowed himself to be manipulated, even though he'd been exposed to some masters of manipulation, like his mother and Lucinda.

And finally, after all those lonely years of walking his own path, he saw what the reward was.

Jessica, a woman who had walked her own way as surely as he had. Who had suffered, and come out, not beaten, but better.

"Will you say my goodbyes to Michelle?"

So, as he suspected, Michelle had only been a stepping-stone for Lucinda. Still, he nodded, left a big tip for the poor waitress, and escorted Lucinda into the mall. He noticed a jewelry store right across from the restaurant.

He must have looked a little too eager, because Lucinda's lips twisted upward wryly. "Brian, you have it bad!"

"Yeah," he said and jutted out his chin. "I do."

She grabbed his arm and dragged him over to a display case. A sign on top of it read Engaging Moments By Henri.

"Oh, I love Henri jewelry. It's exquisite. I suppose she'll be getting something that looks like that," she said a trifle bitterly.

He looked through the case at where she had pointed. He laughed. "No, I don't think so. I'm a cop, not the CEO of Microsoft. She wouldn't like that anyway. It would be more like this."

Lucinda leaned close to the case where he had tapped on the glass. When she straightened, her eyes held the light of defeat.

"How cute," she said, never one to give in gracefully.

The ring wasn't cute. It was tasteful and simple and lovely, just like Jessica.

She reached up and touched his cheek. "Brian," she said softly, hoarsely. "I wish you happiness."

"Thank you," he said, not without suspicion.

And then she stood on tiptoe and kissed him very tenderly on the mouth. He was amazed a man could be kissed like that and not feel one little thing—not the faintest stirring of desire. When he put her away from him without responding, she laughed and tossed her hair. At least three men nearly walked into walls when she did that. He knew she was going to be okay.

"Just testing," she said, and then pulled her sunglasses over her eyes, turned on her high heels and walked quickly away, appreciative male gazes following her.

He lost no time in getting back to the rings. "That one," he said to the clerk, moments later.

"A lovely choice."

"Thanks." Lucinda, as always, had missed the essence of the ring. It was just like Jessica, a band of pure gold with one winking multifaceted diamond radiating light from its center.

He came out of the store feeling like he was floating on cloud nine. It was the first time spending a month's salary on something he could carry in a teeny bag had ever made him feel that good.

"Hey, Michelle," he called, when he saw her in the distance with her friends, but she mustn't have heard him because she just kept walking.

He'd come back and get her later. With Jessica. Together they'd give her the happy news.

Jessica lay on her couch with a cold cloth on her head, feeling very much as if she'd been the one who had consumed too much of Aunt Hetty's brandy.

Lucinda, of course, had waltzed out of here this morning without a readily discernable trace of a hangover or remorse.

Lucinda in her house. The nerve of that man! Not only had he not told her about Lucinda being Michelle's godmother, and therefore irrevocably linked to his life forever, he had dumped her here.

And she'd heard all of Lucinda's plans for him. What chance did she have if Lucinda wanted him?

O'Henry whined and licked her fingers.

"Oh, yeah," Jessica told him. "When Lucinda Potter crooks her finger, you and I come dead last."

Michelle had wanted to take her pup with them this morning, but Lucinda had not wanted her car to smell like a dog. How could Brian tolerate a woman like that?

"I bet she doesn't like your truck, either," she said to the ceiling, adjusting her washcloth on her forehead.

Jessica, a voice inside her said, *you are not going to take this lying down. If you want him, fight for him.*

"Who would want him?" she asked out loud. But the deeper part of her answered. So, he hadn't told her about Lucinda. That didn't mean he loved the woman.

How could he have any feelings at all for Lucinda, when he had chased, her, Jessica, through the forest yesterday? Kissed her? Held her? Who had he called, last night after that crisis was resolved? Not Lucinda.

She wasn't taking it lying down. Not this time. She was getting to the bottom of this. She swung her feet off the couch and got up with determination. She was giving him a chance to explain himself. She was giving herself a chance to believe she was the better woman.

Unfortunately, she hadn't videotaped Lucinda's drunken snores last night, but if he needed that kind of convincing it would probably be better to let him go.

She went into a flurry of activity in her bedroom, selecting just the right outfit, a white knit top and matching shorts. She moussed her hair into some semblance of order when the phone rang. *Him*, she hoped. But if it wasn't, that was okay. She wasn't waiting in the wings this time!

"Hello?"

"J-J-Jessica?"

The confusion stopped roiling within her, replaced instantly with concern. "Michelle? Where are you. What's wrong?"

The girl was obviously crying. "H-h-he's going to marry her."

Until that moment, Jessica had been mad at him. He hadn't, after all, told her about Lucinda's ongoing involvement in his life.

But she had been willing to believe that he was a poor communicator, not a bad person. She had been willing to believe in herself—that she had become a woman who could make good choices, who could be trusted to know a good man from a bad one. Now, that belief wavered, washed in the light of doubt.

Brian was that dumb, was he? That he'd throw his life away on a miserable wretch of a woman? She drank too much and she was superficial, self-centered and cynical.

And gorgeous. Wasn't that all that mattered to men?

Now who was being cynical?

But at least this time, she thought, she was placing the blame where it belonged. There would be no finding herself wanting or looking for the reason she had failed to win Brian Kemp all over again!

"How do you know that?" Jessica asked Michelle, striving for calm. Her moment of righteousness was dissolving into sadness. No, something beyond sadness. A place gray and endless, without a top and without a bottom, a grief so great it would devour her, if she allowed it.

"I saw them together. Shopping at the mall. At the engagement ring counter. They picked one out and then he k-k-kissed her."

Jessica was silent. The enormity of the betrayal seemed like more than she could handle. Just yesterday he had been kissing her, his lips full of wild promise. And today he'd been kissing Lucinda. Shopping for rings with her?

Reassure, Michelle, she ordered herself through the haze of her pain. But what could she say? It may not have been what it appeared? A kiss at the engagement ring counter was not likely to be anything except what it appeared.

Be strong, she ordered herself. "Michelle, how wonderful for you. You're going to have a family again."

Saying the words was like putting a knife into her own chest. For the family that she had been dreaming of had not had anything to do with Lucinda. No, her fantasy family had babies and dogs and ponies. And Michelle.

And her and Brian together. Forever.

"You're my family," Michelle wailed. "You and O'Henry. I hate Uncle Brian and I hate her."

How could Jessica tell her not to hate her uncle, when she felt so distressed with herself? And what could she say about Lucinda that wasn't totally damning?

"She's beautiful," she muttered lamely.

Michelle snorted. "She's like Bambi, only with a brain, which is twice as dangerous. And *her* implants are within the legal limit."

Jessica could not encourage Michelle to be catty, even if what she most wanted was to join in. Instead, she changed the subject. "Where are you?"

"At the mall. But I'm just leaving."

"No. I'll come get you," Jessica decided. "We'll talk about it."

"No."

"Come on, sweetie, it's going to be okay." She knew she did not sound the least bit convincing because she herself was not convinced.

Her whole world was crumbling. How could she tell Michelle everything was going to be okay?

"It's not going to be okay," Michelle said, her voice much more sure than Jessica's had been. "I can't have Lucinda for a mother. I just can't. She'll always be trying to do my hair and fix my makeup and telling me what to wear, as if I'm some loser."

"Maybe she just cares about you," Jessica said lamely.

"She cares about herself, just like…" but Michelle never finished the sentence.

She didn't have to. Jessica knew exactly what she was thinking. *Just like her mom.* "Michelle, you stay right where you are. I can be there in fifteen minutes."

"Don't bother, because I'm running away."

And then the phone went dead in Jessica's hands. She sank down on the floor, stared at the dead receiver and began to shake uncontrollably.

She realized she did not have the luxury of sitting there shaking. She had to find Michelle before she got too far from the mall.

She shoved her feet in her sandals, picked up her handbag and ran out the door.

* * *

Brian had not been this nervous since the drama teacher had made the mistake of casting him for a small role in *South Pacific*.

He rehearsed his lines now as he had then.

"Jessica, I love you madly. Won't you be my wife?"

They sounded as lame and as stilted as the ones he had rehearsed all those years ago. He recalled how the audience had laughed, and it had not been a funny line.

He didn't want Jessica to laugh. He tried again. "Jessica, I have fallen in love with you. Would you marry me?"

He sounded like an idiot. Like a robot! None of his real feeling seemed to be coming through. Now what? He was heading hell-bent up the highway, a ring on the seat beside him, and he didn't have a clue how to propose!

Brian was about halfway to the turnoff to her place when he saw Jessica's little red truck coming toward him fast. He put his hand out the window and flagged her.

She pulled over onto the shoulder, hopped out of her truck and came running across the highway. A car had to screech its brakes to keep from hitting her.

He frowned as she raced around to the passenger side of the truck.

She looked like hell, her hair kind of half done and half not, her eyes puffy, her face drawn.

And hell on her was gorgeous. It made her look sweet and vulnerable and like she needed him to take her in his arms and make her world all right.

The bag from the jewelry store was on the seat beside him, and he quickly picked it up and shoved it in the glove box. That was a surprise he wasn't willing to reveal until the circumstances were perfect, until he knew just what words to say.

"Michelle just called me from the mall," she said, climbing in the door and slamming it. "Get there quick."

"But I just left there. Michelle was with her friends."

"Drive!"

He was turning the truck around, even as he was asking, "What's wrong?"

"Brian, she said she was running away from home!"

"What? No, you must have misunderstood her. Things have never been better between us." He remembered her laughing as he had swung her around this morning. "Well, maybe she was a little mad at me for playing down the call I went to last night."

"Brian, I didn't misunderstand her, and it wasn't about your call. It was about Lucinda. Once Michelle gets out of that mall, how are we going to find her? What is she going to do?"

"What about her and Lucinda?" he said grimly.

Jessica looked straight ahead. "She said you were kissing Lucinda and choosing engagement rings. She said she couldn't live with Lucinda as a mother."

The need to make haste aside, he slammed on the brakes and swerved onto the shoulder of the road. He took Jessica's chin in his hands and made her look at him. Her green eyes swam with pain.

"Listen up. I am not marrying Lucinda. Ever. You have to believe me."

Everything was going wrong! This wasn't how he'd planned his proposal. He couldn't just ask her, on the side of the road in the middle of a crisis while he was defending himself against her suspicion.

He had it all planned! They were going to be in her garden. He was going to be on bended knee.

"So Michelle manufactured that kiss?" she asked, her voice chilly.

"No. There was a kiss. Lucinda. Not me." Maybe this whole idea had been bad from the beginning.

"I thought it took two people to kiss."

"She kissed me without my permission!"

"It must be terribly hard for you having women throw themselves at you like that."

"Believe me, it is," he said tersely.

"I believe you," she said insincerely. "Please get to the mall."

He cursed. He was dragging Michelle out of that mall by her ear. After he'd lambasted her about drawing all the wrong conclusions and nearly wrecking his life by doing so, he would lambaste Jessica. How could he even be thinking of marrying a woman with so little trust in him? A woman so set in believing the worst of him that she was willing to convict him on very flimsy evidence?

Though, maybe Michelle witnessing that kiss wasn't what either of them would consider flimsy evidence.

He was going to be very glad when this part of the courtship was over. All the uncertainty, all the fretting, all the wondering what to say and how to say it. He was back to Plan A. As soon as they found Michelle, they were going to Jessica's. He was locking Michelle in the house with her dog, and then he would find the prettiest place in the garden and propose to Jessica.

But an hour later, he was feeling very shaken. He and Jessica had been through the mall with a fine-tooth comb. Michelle was not there.

"Call her friends next?" Jessica asked, her animosity toward him forgotten, or at least put temporarily on hold.

It amazed him how well they worked together, even under these most difficult circumstances. "We'll go to her friends' houses, instead of calling. They might tell me she wasn't there on the phone, but I don't think they'd lie to my face. I'll put the word out with parents, too."

"We're going to find her," Jessica said firmly. He felt grateful to her for her largeness of spirit. She actually reached out to comfort him, when he had brought her so damned little comfort in the last twenty-four hours.

He touched his forehead to hers, and the perfect moment he had planned for his declaration was forgotten. "Jessica," he said softly. "It's not Lucinda I want to marry. It's not Lucinda I love."

He was like a plane in a nosedive, building momentum as he fell toward earth, having a hell of a time pulling himself out. This was not the moment!

Chapter Ten

In that moment, when Brian touched his forehead to hers, it seemed as if Jessica understood every secret of the universe, every single thing that was sacred between a man and a woman. She understood questions she did not even know she had asked. She understood the deepest parts of herself.

And then, too soon and too abruptly, he pulled away from her.

"What did you say?" Jessica asked, struggling to understand what had just happened, to put it in perspective. He had said he was not marrying Lucinda; he had said it was not Lucinda he loved.

He had implied more. That he *was* getting married, that he *did* love.

Her soul had heard his love was for her. It had recognized it fully and deeply in that moment of wonder when he had caressed her forehead with his own.

Still, her mind was purely human. Her mind wanted to hear the words! "What did you say?" she asked again.

"Nothing." He stepped back from her, refused to look at her. He ran a hand through the dark strands of his hair. "Forget I said anything. Or if I said something, I shouldn't have. My timing's bad. Story of my life. My thirteen-year-old niece is missing, and nobody knows better than me what happens to thirteen-year-old runaways, and I'm…"

He was beating himself up, and the words were piling up, one on top of the other, and Jessica was getting no closer to the truth. She put her finger over his lips.

"Stop," Jessica commanded him quietly.

She gazed into the depths of those melted-chocolate eyes and saw the amazing truth.

She saw strength and tenderness residing side by side. She saw courage at odds with a certain endearing romantic clumsiness. She saw his worry for his niece, but she saw, too, that his hope was greater than his fear. She saw, in his eyes, that he hoped for great things.

And so she would trust him, and she would believe in herself. When he was ready, he would tell her the secret his eyes had already revealed.

"Let's go find Michelle," she said.

Grateful, he took her hand in his and squeezed it. She felt the truth. And she saw it again as they enlarged and photocopied the wallet picture he had of Michelle. She saw it as they headed downtown and talked to the street kids. She saw his blend of tenderness and toughness. She saw it as he held himself together with each patrol car that they pulled over and gave a picture to. She saw it in the way he kept sliding her looks, the truth so naked in his eyes she wondered why she had ever thought she needed words.

All of her life, Jessica had seen what others could not. She had always been able to see the healing power of pure love.

Now, she understood the challenge she had been given—to accept that gift for herself. A long time ago, when her parents had died, she had lost her ability to trust. When Brian had disappointed her, years later, it had seemed to confirm that earlier message: Love, of the earthly variety, would hurt her.

But now, she understood that not loving was to not live fully. She understood trust and love were woven together in ways that could not be split. Jessica had thought all along that it was about whether or not she could trust Brian.

Now, she saw it in a totally different light. It wasn't about that at all. It was about whether or not she could trust herself.

It was about trusting her heart.

The evidence said he had deceived her about Lucinda. But her heart said he had not. The light in his eyes said he had not. The man who had just talked to those homeless children was not a man who would betray anyone willingly.

When Jessica looked at the man sitting next to her on the worn seat of that old truck, she saw that he was incapable of deception. She had to trust that even though it seemed irrational to do so.

She lived in a world where people were skeptical of anything but the concrete. But weren't the most important things the ones you could not see and could not touch? The things you felt with your heart, and knew with your soul, though there was no proof of their existence?

Had she not lived by rules others did not always understand?

Wasn't it irrational to lay your hands on a sick dog and expect he would be healed?

But doubt did not enter her when she did those things, and she could feel the doubt easing from her now, being replaced with a crystal-clear certainty.

"Brian, why didn't you tell me about Lucinda coming?"

He didn't look like he wanted to jump out of the truck at her probing. He looked relieved. "Aw, Jessica, you got to understand that all my life I've had an absolute gift for failing people, especially women. I've been saddled with this fear of not being good enough, of failing to make others happy. I wanted to make you happy. I couldn't see how announcing Lucinda's impending arrival was going to do that."

"Why don't you tell me about some of those other times?" she suggested softly. "That you tried to make people happy?"

And so as they drove around, he told her. About a mother who had always wanted him to be what he could not: quiet, controllable, conservative. About the girls and young women who had come to him with their neediness, and how he had let them down.

"I think I just started ducking out from people's disappointment," he said finally. "I hid out in football and old trucks and my work, creating this whole safe world, where I could make mistakes, and nobody would cry over them."

He took a long breath. "I never learned to say the words that really make a man a man. Like I'm sorry. I made a mistake." He took another long breath. He pulled over the truck. He took her hands and looked deep into her eyes.

"Lucinda and I had a relationship during high school. We were engaged once, briefly. After Kevin and Amanda's funeral we were both lonely and hurt and I think we both considered taking it somewhere else.

"She would have been the safest kind of woman for me, Jessica. I wouldn't have ever had to connect deeply enough for her to hurt me.

"And I might have accepted that once in my life. Maybe. If I hadn't met you. I found out, all over again, just like that first night we met, what really connecting with another person is like. After you've shared what you and I have had, don't you think you could die of loneliness if you accepted anything less than that?"

Jessica nodded. She had felt these words coming before he spoke them. They were something she could breathe in, each one becoming a part of her and blossoming within her like the flowers in her garden.

"I've been dying of loneliness since that night I first met you, looking for that feeling in all the wrong places. I was trying to become a man worthy of that feeling. And then when you were brought back to me, I didn't want to do anything wrong. But I did, and I'm sorry. I'm sorry I did things wrong when Lucinda came. I'm sorry if the mistakes I made hurt you."

Jessica saw only strength and sincerity in his apology. Gently, she said, "Your apology is accepted. And I offer one of my own: I'm sorry I didn't trust you, Brian. It's written all over you the kind of man you are, and I chose to believe something else because of my own insecurities."

As she spoke those words, Jessica could feel a familiar sensation of light within her. She closed her eyes, even as they filled with tears. She let the light grow until its tingling radiance filled her up.

She finally accepted the gift for herself. The gift was love, pure, strong, and capable of creating miracles and healing hurts.

And in that moment of light, she knew the answer to the puzzle they were trying so desperately to solve. There would be time later to explore the beauty of the experience that was growing between them. But first, all the fears had to be laid to rest, each and everyone.

For if love had an enemy, it was fear.

"Michelle's gone home," Jessica said. "We'll find her at my place."

"How would she get there?" Brian asked. "There's no bus, it's a million miles from anywhere."

"She's there," Jessica said with quiet certainty.

"Okay," Brian said. "I believe it. While we've been combing these streets, she's probably been sitting out at your place smelling the flowers."

And he turned the truck around, and they headed for home.

But when they got there, dusk was gathering, and there were no lights on in the cottage. The gardens were way too quiet. There was no movement at all.

"She's not here," Brian said flatly.

But Jessica was certain. She went in the house, room to room, Brian close behind her. What was missing?

"O'Henry!" she said. "Where's O'Henry?"

They both shot to the back door and called. And they both heard the piteous whine at the same time.

The dog normally would have run to them, but in the growing darkness, they could see he was laying outside the garden shed, refusing to give up his post. His head was on his paws, and he looked particularly forlorn.

Brian let out a huge sigh of relief.

"She's in there. She probably didn't let the dog in with her because she knew we'd notice the dog missing and find her."

"She had no idea how loyal he was going to be," Jessica agreed, grinning, feeling as if the sun shone inside of her even as the moon rose outside of her.

"Let's leave her in there over night," Brian said, letting some of the aggravation he felt finally show. "That would serve her right."

Jessica shook her head. "I can't punish her for taking after you."

"Taking after me? As if I would hide in a garden shed!"

"She runs away from the things that hurt her. She saw you kissing Lucinda and it hurt her, and scared her."

"Okay, okay. She doesn't have to spend the night in the shed. Jessica, you have always asked me to be the better man."

Together they went to the garden shed and opened the door. Michelle was squished way into the back corner, her knees up to her chest, crying silently.

Jessica was not sure she had ever seen a girl who more wanted to be found.

Instead of asking her to come out, Brian got down on his hands and knees. He crawled through the tangle of garden equipment and over the dirt until he arrived at Michelle. And then he gathered her in his arms and cradled her against his chest like a baby.

If Jessica had even the smallest doubt left about who he was, it was gone now, evaporating completely after seeing the way he held that child.

She crawled into the shed, sat down on the dirty floor beside Brian, laid her head on his shoulder and touched Michelle's hair. O'Henry came in and, after sampling the tears on Michelle's cheeks, he sighed and laid his head on Jessica's lap.

None of them said anything, not a single word. For some things do not need words: profound gratitude.

Pure love.

Darkness came and wrapped itself around them and finally Michelle spoke.

"I'm sorry I made you worry about me."

"It's okay," Brian said. "I'm expecting a few more gray hairs, compliments of you, along the way. Just tell me why you ran away instead of coming to me. Talking to me."

"Lucinda is so much like my mother it scares me," she whispered. "I can't live like that anymore. Unkie, I like living with you better than I liked living with my mom and dad. I feel so guilty about it, I want to hate you."

"Aw, sugar," he said tenderly.

"They made all the money in the world, but they didn't have time for me. They never did anything they said they would, even if they promised. They drank all the time and went to parties. I never had to tell them where I was or who I was with. They never told me what time to be home. My mom only noticed me if I was wearing something she didn't like."

Jessica bit back the urge to tell her it wasn't true, but it was so obvious from her voice how true it was. Besides, Brian seemed to be handling it magnificently, soaking up her pain just by listening and not loosening his hold on her.

"And then I came to live with you, and you make all these dumb rules, and question my friends' mothers and are hardly ever mean back even when I'm mean to you. Even when I dyed my hair black you never told me how ugly it was. I mean, when I tell you I hitchhiked out here, you're going to ground me for a month, aren't you?"

He swore. "A month? Try a year! You hitchhiked out here?"

"See," Michelle said with satisfaction. "You care."

"If you hitchhiked out here I'm going to care all right. Right across your behind."

Michelle actually giggled. "A friend's mom drove me out."

"Are you ever lucky," he told her sternly.

"Everything's going to change if you marry Aunt Lucy. I love her, but I don't like her very much."

She turned her face into his chest and cried while he stroked her hair.

"Michelle, I'm not marrying Lucinda."

"Don't lie to me! I can figure things out! I'm not a baby!"

"Okay," he said gently. "You tell me what you figured out."

"I didn't get to come for lunch because you were going to pop the question. I saw you looking at rings. I saw you kiss her in the middle of the mall as if nobody was watching. I saw you walk out of there with a bag."

"I bought something at the jewelry store. But it wasn't for Lucinda. Do you want to see what it was? I'd like to show it to you."

"You want to show whatever you bought to me?" Michelle asked. "Is it for me?"

"Nope. I just need to know if you approve of it. Not you," Brian said to Jessica. "You have to go in the house for a while."

Jessica shook her head and tried to feel offended, but could not. She kissed the top of Michelle's head, met his eyes over her hair and wondered if she had ever felt so gloriously happy or complete.

Her turn was coming. Her second chance at love.

And she was taking it.

Brian slung his arm companionably over Michelle's shoulder and walked with her out to the truck. Once there, he opened the glove compartment and retrieved the bag inside it.

"Open it," he said to Michelle.

She gave him a questioning look, but then opened the bag and stared wide-eyed at the velvet box. Her eyes went very round as she lifted the lid. She touched the ring with her fingertip, then frowned.

"I thought you said it wasn't an engagement ring."

"No, that's not what I said. I said it wasn't for Lucinda."

A small and lovely smile tickled Michelle's lips. She looked up at the stars and squeezed her eyes tight together, like a small child making a wish, or maybe one thanking their guardian angel for a prayer answered. And then she opened her eyes and looked at the ring once more.

"Oh," she breathed. "I get it, Uncle Brian. This is not the kind of ring Lucinda would like. Not at all. I know exactly who would like a ring like this."

There was a new openness in her young face when she flung her arms around his middle and hugged him hard.

He realized as he held her and the stars winked on one by one that he had been in the process of becoming a better man for a long, long time. Somewhere along the line of his life, as unlikely as it seemed, he had became a man worthy of the trust of a young girl.

A man worthy of the love of a woman like Jessica Moran.

"I need some help," he said.

"Anything."

For a moment, he thought he might take her up on that long ago offer to be his romance coach.

But he realized, suddenly, he didn't need that kind of help. He knew exactly what to do. He'd known all along.

He just hadn't ever met a woman he had wanted to do it for. All his life, Brian felt women had made demands on him. Make me happy, make me feel, do more, be more. As if they were somehow incomplete and he was supposed to be the missing piece of the puzzle.

And then there was Jessica. Who had done all that needed doing for herself. Who made no demands on him.

And because of that, he had a sudden desire to make her happy, to make her feel delirious with joy, to do more than he had ever done and be more than he had ever been.

"Could you take the hose and fill up the pond for me? I have to run back into town for a minute. And when you're done filling the pond, keep Jessica in the house, away from the windows."

"How am I supposed to do that?"

"Explain football to her?" he said hopefully. His niece had a surprising grasp for the game and a genuine enthusiasm for it.

It was a long time later when his preparations were finally done. He glanced at his watch. Midnight. Perhaps an odd time for a proposal.

And perhaps not. From the moment he had entered this garden and reentered Jessica's life he had been in the grip of an enchantment. What better time to complete the spell that was being woven than the stroke of midnight?

Taking a deep breath, Brian surveyed his handiwork and knew he could do no more. Now he had to trust that the enchantment had worked as hard on her as it had on him. He went and knocked on the door of the cottage, and Michelle answered.

"Any luck with football?" he asked his niece, ruffling her hair.

"Forget it. You'll have to learn to play Scrabble." She looked over his shoulder and smiled. "Oh, Uncle Brian, that is so cool. Jessica."

Then Jessica was peeking out at him, suddenly shy, and he extended his hand to her. She took it, and he led her into the garden. Michelle took one last look, sighed, then turned around and shut the door, leaving them alone.

With Jessica's hand in his, he turned and surveyed his handiwork. He had transformed her yard. Torches illuminated the waters of the recently filled pond. Dozens of candle flames flickered and leaped and sparked, bright as fairies, among the flowers. The darkness was chased away by the strength of those softly burning lights, just as the darkness had been chased from his soul by the softly burning light of Jessica.

"Oh," she said, looking around. Her eyes filled with tears.

Taking a tight hold of her hand, he led her to the bench beside the pond and settled her on it.

"Brian, it's so beautiful," she gasped.

"Shh," he said. "I'll forget my lines."

But when he got down on bended knee before her, her tears, painted in gold from the softly flickering lights, made him forget his lines anyway.

"I should have written them down," he muttered, but then he caught her gaze, more gold than green in the subdued light, and he knew he didn't have to write anything down.

Instead, he just said the words that came to his heart.

"Jessica," he said, "life is a balancing act. Sometimes you make others happy. Sometimes you make yourself happy. Sometimes you're lucky enough to do both.

"I think being married is finding somebody compatible enough that the third one happens the most often."

It sounded just right to him, as real and as genuine as he knew how to make it. Still on bended knee, he reached into his shirt pocket and took out the ring box. He opened the lid and held the box out to her.

"This is a symbol of my love for you," he said, and found his voice hoarse. "Jessica, will you marry me? Will you be my wife?"

She took the box, but she didn't look at what was inside of it.

She looked, instead, at what was inside of him.

"Yes," she whispered.

He couldn't believe his ears. "What did you say?"

"Nothing," she teased him. "Forget I said anything. Or if I said something, I shouldn't have. My timing's bad. Story of my life."

She was playing with the most romantic moment of his life?

"Are you going to be this infuriating all our lives?" he demanded.

"Our lives? In order for there to be an *our*, I'd have to say yes and I haven't done that yet."

There was no doubt, from the way she said that, exactly what she planned to answer when she got around to it.

He carefully put the ring aside then. And then he scooped her up, ignoring her squeal of protest, and waded right out into the center of the pond.

"Say yes!" he ordered.

She laughed into his shoulder, helplessly.

"Say yes," he warned her.

The door of the cottage opened.

"Has he asked yet?" Michelle called.

"Yes," Jessica called back.

"What did you say?" Michelle shouted.

"I said yes!"

"You did not!" Brian sputtered, trying to make himself heard over Michelle's squeals. "You were stringing me along. You were probably going to make me wait until dawn."

"I've waited fourteen years for this second chance. You could wait a few minutes!"

"Hey! You said yes?" he asked.

"I said yes," she confirmed.

He laughed. He spun her around crazily until the water splashed up all around them. He took her lips in his, until the world spun dizzily.

The dog hit him right in the knees and they both went over with a splash. Their lips never came apart. O'Henry nearly drowned them both, swimming anxiously back and forth to share his kisses.

And then Michelle arrived at the pond, surveyed the scene affectionately, and with a shake of her head, walked right into the moonlit pool, too. In the blink of an eye, they were all chasing each other through the water, splashing and laughing hysterically.

"We're never going to be a normal family, are we?" Michelle asked happily, an hour later, wrapped in a blanket and sipping cocoa.

The truth was Brian was not sure what normal was. Was it

what his mother had wanted for him? Was "normal" the life of outward success and inner emptiness his brother had led?

If it was either of those things, he would choose splashing around in a pond at midnight anytime.

Michelle went to bed, and, after all the excitement and exhaustion of her day, she fell asleep during good-night hugs and kisses. Jessica and Brian stood, arms looped around each other's waists, watching the sleeping child and the dog.

"Brian?" Jessica whispered.

"Yes, Jessica?"

"I love you madly."

"I figured it out."

"I'm going to marry you."

"Thank God."

"And we are going to have babies."

"I hoped."

"Here's to second chances," she said. She took his hand and led him into the hall, then gently shut Michelle's door behind them. He opened his arms, and Jessica came into them. He folded them around her and marveled at the sensation of homecoming.

Normal? Who would want normal when they could have this? An enchantment, a place where an ordinary man could find royalty within himself, a place so beyond normal it bordered on pure magic.

He kissed her, and he knew finally the spell was complete, frog to prince.

Against her hair, he said, "Here's to happily-ever-after."

* * * * *

If you enjoyed what you just read,
then we've got an offer you can't resist!

Take 2 bestselling love stories FREE!

Plus get a FREE surprise gift!

HARLEQUIN® flipside™

It's all about me!

Coming in July 2004,

Harlequin Flipside heroines tell you exactly what they think...in their own words!

WHEN SIZE MATTERS
by Carly Laine
Harlequin Flipside #19

WHAT PHOEBE WANTS
by Cindi Myers
Harlequin Flipside #20

I promise these first-person tales will speak to you!

**Look for Harlequin Flipside
at your favorite retail outlet.**

Rediscover the remarkable O'Hurley family...

#1 *New York Times* bestselling author

NORA ROBERTS

BORN O'HURLEY

Starring her mesmerizing family of Irish performers in America.

The unique upbringing of the O'Hurley triplet sisters and their mysterious older brother has led to four extraordinary lives. This collector's-size edition showcases the stories of Abby and Maddy O'Hurley.

Available in August 2004.

Where love comes alive™